Matt Shaw Publications

D1519486

A Note from the Author:

Sometimes I miss the simplicity of horror stories. These days they have a tendency to try and make things overcomplicated with far-fetched plots and ridiculous villains, both of which do nothing but to detract from the whole fun of the horror. Everything has to have a reason, everything has to make sense, and everything has to wrap up nicely. And sometimes that's right. They do need to make sense, they do need reasons, and they do need to all tie-in together in a neat little package by the end of it but sometimes, just sometimes, I don't think it's necessarily a bad thing to pay homage to the old horrors of the late seventies and early eighties. I've done it before - with my story Consumed - and I loved every minute of it. The people who read the notes at the start and took the story for what it was meant to be also seemed to enjoy it so now I wanted to do the same again to the old cannibal tribe stories I used to see in supposedly banned films back in the late seventies (not that I watched them then for I hadn't yet been born). The main one that lodged in my brain when I watched the previously banned movies, which had been given a new lease of life by having their bans lifted in the early nineties, was Cannibal Holocaust. I remember watching it trying to figure out what the fuss was about. In fact, when I first watched it, it actually annoyed me with the silly plot and over the top gore which just looked too fake. It was only years later that I came to appreciate what the filmmakers had been doing. They were simply trying to make a video nasty. They wanted the notoriety that went along with such films and they earned it. So well done them.

As previously mentioned you don't tend to get stories like that anymore and I do think that is a shame. Sure I wouldn't want Grindhouse films - or stories - all of the time but once in a blue moon… Why not? Why shouldn't we disengage our brains once in a while and go for the fun ride these stories have to offer?

Well… It's a blue moon now because… That is what I have attempted to do with this story. I have attempted to bring some of the essence of those stories back. I have attempted to tell a story where you can switch off from the real world, not really have to think, and just go for the fun ride on offer.

And, with that in mind, I hope you enjoy it.

Kind Regards,

Matt Shaw

www.facebook.com/mattshawpublications
www.mattshawpublications.co.uk

ASHES

MATT SHAW

A "TASTE" of things to come:

It's a different world to what you're used to. The locals have their own way of life. It's a way that some - from other parts of the world - may frown upon but, to them, it is perfectly acceptable. Not just that, it is a necessity designed to protect their ways. What little clothes they wear are washed in rivers of brown water. Time is not taken up with computer consoles, sports, or reading but rather hunting and surviving. The men hunt, the men prepare the food, the women ensure it cooks to a standard befitting a king or, in this instance, a Chief. The children watch on, taking in all that must be learned. For example, **how to cook the perfect piece of meat**.

First of all the body is **stripped**. Under garments - the bottom half and top half - and footwear are offered up to the Chief or his wife. If they do not fit or they don't take a shine to them, they are offered to next high ranking tribesman; in this instance the witch-doctor. Once the body is **naked** it is laid upon the ground with its arms and legs spread in a **starfish position**. What comes next takes not one but five people. One holds the left arm, one secures the right, and the other two take a leg each. The fifth controls the **sharpened pole**.

The pole is seven foot in length and made from wood. Both ends are sharpened to fine points. Only when the other four people have taken **a hold of the limbs** does the fifth person take the pole and **slowly insert it** into the meat. If the meat is male, the pole slides in **via the rectum** - pushing up and **piercing through the inner stomach**. As the pole moves up through the inside of the body, the two people holding the arms raise the body up so that the head tilts back. With the head tilted back, the pole easily finds its way along the neck **and out of the mouth**. The same process is followed if the **meat is female**. The only difference is that the pole enters the body **via the vagina**. Once the pole is pushed completely through to the other end, one of the other helpers will take a hold of the end **sticking from** the mouth and give it a tug until an equal amount is visible at **both ends of the meat**. With the pole in place, the arms and legs are tied to the body with pieces of vine and the meat is then lifted between all people and placed over a fire where it is **cooked for a couple of hours.** Sometimes the vines will tear and the limbs will dangle closer to the flames. These are either left and served as 'well done', or - when they're ready sooner than the rest of the meal - cut from the body with a swing of a machete. During the cooking process, two of the cooks will occasionally turn the meat to ensure it is **cooked evenly throughout**.

With the exception of being stripped off, Corinna knew nothing of this. Her sweaty, naked body struggling in the strong midday heat as four of the tribesmen held her in position. She knew nothing of what was to come but could guess everything. She screamed at them to stop. She begged them to release her but her words were formed in a language unlearned by her captors. Even so she didn't stop calling out. She didn't stop pleading for her life. Pained screams of fear, frustration, and anger and fruitless kicks of her legs, held firm in the hands of strong men. She tilted her head up and screamed once more as another approached with a long pole of thick wood, sharpened at the tip, clutched in his dark hands. She lashed out again, trying to shake the unwanted hands from her limbs. The man with the pole barked something to his fellow tribesmen. A strange language; a series of clicks of the tongue and sounds which could only be described as 'noise' to the uneducated ear.

"Fuck you!" Corinna screamed out as they each pinned her harder to the dirt covered ground, close by to the roaring fire. She watched, in horror, as the man with the pole came closer - edging it up between her legs with a steady, firm hand. Corinna turned to her watching, powerless friends. A desperate scream for them to do something despite knowing they were in no position to do so. Her friends both bound to large stakes planted deep into the hard ground. All they could do was watch on in horror and worry that they'd be next. One of them - a lad - closed his eyes tight, unable to watch. His mind focusing on the one song playing through in his petrified head…

Lollipop Lollipop

Oh Lolli Lolli Lolli

Lollipop Lollipop

Oh Lolli Lolli Lolli

Lollipop Lollipop

Oh Lolli Lolli Lolli

Lollipop *POP*

Sweeter than candy on a stick

Huckleberry, cherry, or lime

If you have a choice he'd be your pick

But Lollipop is mine...

Corinna's scream changed in pitch as the stake entered her vagina, tearing up the insides as it continued deeper. It pressed against the cervix and she let out another yelp and scream as - one hard push later - it ripped through that too and further inside her.

Lollipop Lollipop

Oh Lolli Lolli Lolli

Lollipop Lollipop

Oh Lolli Lolli Lolli

Lollipop Lollipop

Oh Lolli Lolli Lolli

Lollipop *POP*

Two Days Prior…

1.

"Every fucking night, seriously." Jack was sitting with his three friends: Holly, Stuart,
and Corinna. His eyes were fixed dead ahead, staring at a stage a few tables away from
where they were trying to enjoy a game of cards. A painfully bad rendition of the old
classic tune 'Lollipop' was being blasted out by three female singers who'd somehow
managed to get employed as the resort's entertainment troupe. Part of it at least. The other
group of talentless 'fuck-wits' (as named by Jack) was in the far corner of the room
keeping children entertained with, he guessed, balloon animals. On the first day of their
vacation, they had found it funny when the 'entertainment' took centre stage. They had
laughed at how amateurish they had been. One of them (Stuart) even made the joke that
they'd probably only got the job because they were either relatives of the complex
manager or by saying they'd do it for free. On the second day, they had mocked them
further when they took to the stage at the same time of eight o'clock in the evening and
began their 'set' with the same song ('Lollipop') from the first night. By the third day of
the vacation, they realised this was their routine. There was nothing else to it. They come
out, they sing 'Lollipop', they make people (mostly the children) do a conga around the
room, and then warble out such tripe as Celine Dion classics before getting off stage
(thank God) at ten o'clock in the evening. Usually to loud applause which Jack thought

had more to do with the audience being thankful the entertainment had finished rather than having actually enjoyed what they were forced to listen to. 'Forced' being the main word there. The resort was in the middle of nowhere. If they wanted a drink in the evening, they had to sit in this bar. There were no other bars that opened, for some reason, and there were no local establishments nearby that the group could venture to. It was this or sit in the room doing nothing. And this was why Jack, the twenty-six year old adrenaline junkie of the foursome, hated holidays like this. "Like - would it kill them to learn another song?"

"Like what?" Holly asked. Holly was a pretty blonde girl; a year younger than Jack. The couple had been dating for three years now. Holly was also the reason they were on this holiday; a reasonably priced Winter Sun getaway to a volcanic island none of the group had ever heard of before. But then, they didn't need to have heard of it before. They checked the Internet for average temperatures and saw that they were high. High temperatures, low cost holiday. When Holly had mentioned it as an option, there hadn't been much of an argument. With the exception of Jack that is. But after the last holiday he chose for them to go on, he didn't get much of a say this time around. "You don't like the song?" she joked. "I think it's catchy." She started mouthing the words to it in perfect timing with the group on stage.

"That's the problem. I go to bed - it's in my head. I wake up for a piss in the middle of the night - it's in my head. I wake up in the morning - I'm singing the same fucking song. You know how annoying that is?"

"Nearly as annoying as hearing you moan about this holiday?" Holly replied, quick as a flash. Stuart and Corinna laughed, without taking their eyes from the cards in each of their hands.

Jack immediately got his back up, "Okay - are any of you able to tell me you're really enjoying this trip? I mean, seriously. Hand on heart, would you say you'd come back next year for a repeat of this?"

"It has sun. It has a pool. It has alcohol on tap. I'm good," Stuart said. Stuart was the same age as Jack. The pair had grown up together having met at school. They ended up in the same college, their results were near identical (not the best), and they even ended up being recruited by the same telesales marketing company. They were like two peas in a pod, but after the last holiday, Stuart was glad of a change of pace.

"Hey, Stuart…. Remember when you had some balls?" Jack asked.

Stuart flipped him the finger.

"Look, I know this is your choice, I get that but…" Jack sighed, "Can we please get out and about tomorrow? Please? Do some fucking exploring or something? Honestly, I am going stir-fucking-crazy here. And I swear, I hear this song one more time, I'm going to have to stab someone." He threw his cards down on the table. Regardless of how the rest of the conversation went, he'd had enough of playing it now. There were only so many games of cards a guy could take, especially when they only knew the rules to one game. "Look, I was talking to one of the guys who works here and they were talking about this beach…"

"We have a beach here," Holly interrupted him.

Jack ignored her and continued, "No one goes to this beach. Locals don't bother because hardly any of them drive, and it's a little way away. Tourists don't know about it. Unlike the man-made lagoon here, with its black sands, this one has pure white sand. And he says the water…"

"White sand?" It was Stuart's turn to interrupt him. "It's a volcanic island. The sand will be black."

"Why would he lie? He wasn't selling tickets to this place. White sands and the clearest of water he says we're ever likely to see."

"Can't we just stay here? I just wanted a week of lounging around," Corinna sighed. Corinna was dating Stuart and had gotten to know the rest of the group through her relationship with him. They'd only been dating for a couple of months. A girl of striking beauty. Long dark hair and eyes that seemed to change colour - one minute brown and the next green, depending on the light they were seen in. Unlike the lads who got to sit on the phone all day for work, Corinna found herself running ragged from her job in the retail sector. Some of her friends, who also worked in retail, often complained they were bored during the day but she never seemed to have the time to be bored. Working in one of the busiest ladies shops, in London's Oxford Street, there were always customers milling around needing help or stock to be put out. She was glad that, for once, the holiday they were having was one which involved soaking up the sun and enjoying the tranquility. Especially after the last one. She turned to Holly, "This was what you wanted. Wouldn't you rather stay here?"

"I'm happy to stay here," she said.

The room burst into a round of applause. The 'entertainment' was taking their final bows already. Jack looked around at the zombie-like state of the rest of the holidaymakers and then back to the group, "Please. I need to get out of here. Just one day exploring and then I'll stay quiet for the rest of the trip. I'll happily follow the rest of the sheep, yeah? One day."

"Why don't you two go?" Corinna suggested. She was referring to the boys. If she and Holly were happy to stay behind, it didn't mean they couldn't venture off together.

"It'll be best with all of us," Jack pushed her. "Come on. What do you say? One day?" He looked around the members of the group. He could tell by Stuart's face that he was up for it. The only reason he hadn't said anything was because he didn't want to annoy Corinna. Holly would be easy to win round. It was just down to Corinna - and, if the others said yes, she'd soon buckle under peer pressure.

"And how are we going to get to this beach?" Corinna asked. Just as Jack had realised it was down to her to make the choice, she too realised it.

"He said for a small fee, which I would cover, we could borrow his jeep. Come on, what do you say? You want relaxation? Imagine how relaxed you'll be on this quiet beach. Imagine the warm sea water beckoning you in, the white sands, perfect blue skies…" He held his wrist up revealing a blue wristband supplied by the resort, "You know what this is?"

"Our meal ticket," Corinna said. In a way, it was. The blue wristband was given to guests as they checked into the resort. It let the staff know who was entitled to the all-inclusive food and drink option offered by some of the travel companies.

"It's a restraint keeping us bound to this place. It's their way of controlling where we are. Of course we aren't going to want to go exploring when we might miss out on free food and drink… God, could you imagine? A restraint. Do you like them controlling you because - by putting that on - that's what you're saying. You like to be controlled. You like to be dominated."

"Okay, fine. You cover the cost and I'll do it." Corinna caved. Jack cheered and jumped up from his chair.

"You guys won't regret this," he shouted. "Leave it to me, I'll get everything sorted! This is going to be awesome!"

Corinna turned to the other two and said, "Just so you know - what he just said was bullshit… I'm just fed up with him going on. If it costs us one day out of the resort to keep him quiet for the rest of the trip, that's fine by me."

Holly laughed, "Now you know what I have to put up with."

"Is he always like this?" Corinna asked. They'd been out as a group for social occasions before but this was the first time she'd accompanied them on a proper holiday out of the country. To answer her question, Holly nodded - as did Stuart. Corinna turned to Stuart, "Don't you go getting any ideas."

"You're lucky," Holly said. "Stuart's the level-headed one." She looked at Stuart. He looked away, embarrassed, hoping Corinna wouldn't notice his reaction to the smile of his best friend's girlfriend. What had happened between them was a long time ago. It had been a drunken fling. A silly mistake. One they both promised to bury and yet here we was, thinking about her every time she looked at him. He couldn't help it. As soon as her eyes fixed upon him, he immediately started picturing that look on her face when she had been on her knees, looking up at him - holding eye contact - with his cock between her lips. Holly, unaware of Stuart's X-rated flashback, continued talking to Corinna, "Did you hear about the last holiday? The one Jack organised for us?"

#

Holly's screaming echoed through the mountain tops as she lay back in the thick, white snow. She didn't dare look down. She knew it was bad. She could feel it. She tried to ignore the pain and concentrated on the blue skies directly above her. A few wispy clouds crawling across from the horizon. She attempted to focus on them, turning them from clouds to objects; a cat, a flower... Burning pain... Searing agony... Dog... A funny face... Crutches... Wheelchair... She screamed out again unable to keep pretending everything was okay.

"Holly!" a voice called out. It was Stuart. Holly turned her head to the side and saw him approaching; a genuine look of concern on his face. He skidded to a stop next to where she lay, kicking up some flakes of snow in the process. "Oh fuck!" he noticed her leg. The ski had come away completely and snapped in two. It wasn't the only thing to have snapped. Her leg was also bent at an extreme angle. Tears streamed down her face as she tried to talk to him. No words came out other than pained whimpers. Stuart looked around. "Where's Jack?" The pair had headed down the mountain together. Jack had promised to look out for Holly as - although it wasn't the first time she'd skied - she was nowhere near as experienced as him. Stuart presumed he'd gone off to get help, "Has he gone to get someone?" he asked. Holly shook her head from side to side and screamed again. Stuart quickly took his coat off and laid it across Holly's body in an attempt to keep her warm. He looked around - there was no one. He was fuming with his friend right now. Jack said the two of them would go down the mountain together. Back home, before they came on the trip, he had even made a big thing about how romantic it could have been. Yet - first day up the mountain, he had shot off. No doubt trying to beat his record for getting down the mountain in the quickest time possible. She must have tried to keep up and taken a dive, without him knowing. He dismissed thoughts of Jack from his mind. Now wasn't the time to think about him. He had to worry about Holly and how best to help her. Looking around at the lack of other skiers heading down the hill, he had a horrible thought that he might have to leave her by herself whilst he continued down the mountain to fetch the paramedics. "Listen," he said, "I'm going to go and get help, okay? I'll be a quick as I can."

"Please don't leave me," the pain in her voice broke Stuart's heart and gave him further reason to hate Jack right at this particular moment. He bit his tongue to prevent himself telling Holly what a selfish prick her boyfriend was. "I'm scared," she whimpered.

"I don't have a choice," he said. "I'm sorry. I'll be as quick as I can. You just need to promise me that you won't try and move, okay?"

"I don't want you to leave me," she said - ignoring him. He didn't blame her. Had it been him lying there, he knew there was a chance he'd be begging someone to stay with him too. Yet he knew he had no choice.

"I'll be right back," he promised. "And everything will be okay. Tonight, when you're close to a fire with a blanket over you and a hot drink in your hand, we'll all be laughing about this." Maybe not Jack. He had no right to laugh with them. In Stuart's little fantasy world, not that much time was really being given to it as he tried to comfort his friend, Jack was in stocks out the front of the resort with a large congregation throwing fruits and vegetables at him.

#

Holly shifted in her chair and stretched out her leg as though re-living the last holiday made her, now-mended, bone ache once more. She was still sitting with Corinna and Stuart.

"And it was broken?" Corinna asked. She had been told a lot about the group's escapades but this was the first time anyone had told her this particular story. And she could see why too - it wasn't really a story that made it easy to warm to someone she already struggled to like. From the get go she'd told Stuart she thought Jack was arrogant. More than that - she believed he was in love with himself more than he was with Holly.

Not that she could understand why, as she once told Stuart she thought Holly was beautiful and how she could do much better than Jack. Stuart simply smiled when she said it before changing the subject.

"Which is why," Holly said, "this holiday was my choice and I decided to come somewhere hot and calm."

Corinna leaned forward to the table between them and lifted her small beer from the glass surface, raising it into the air. "Well, for what it's worth, I much prefer your style of holiday! Cheers!" She took a sip from the drink; completely missing the shared looked between Stuart and Holly. It hadn't been too long after she'd had her cast removed that the pair had gotten drunk and she'd given him a proper thank you. Corinna set the glass down when it was empty and turned to Stuart, "I'm feeling pretty tired. I might go to bed. You coming?"

Stuart smiled, "I'm not actually tired. I might just stay up a little longer and chat if that's okay with you?" He quickly turned to Holly, "Unless you're shooting off too?"

"I'm not especially tired either," Holly lied. Despite sleeping in the sun for most of the day, she was feeling shattered but she didn't want to pass up the opportunity to talk to Stuart without the others being around. She felt herself relax more when it was just the two of them. She smiled at him, he smiled back.

"Try not to wake me, okay?" Corinna said as she stood up. She reached into her small handbag, which she picked up from the floor by her feet, and checked she had a room card. "You have a key?" she asked Stuart.

"Yes."

"Okay well try not to stay up all night!" she said. It hadn't been the first time she'd got an earlier night than Stuart. She didn't mind going to bed by herself but it did frustrate her when she struggled to get him up in the morning for breakfast. She leaned down and gave him a little peck on the lips.

"I won't," he said, returning the kiss. He watched as Corinna walked away. When she'd walked from the bar area, he turned back to Holly. "If you want, I can go with Jack tomorrow and you two can stay here?"

"You know he won't be satisfied with that. One for all, and all for one. Remember? It's not worth it. You heard him anyway, we go to his beach tomorrow and he'll keep quiet when we get back. It's a small price to pay and - besides - it might be a nice beach?"

"Well it's up to you. I'm just conscious of the fact it's supposed to be your holiday."

She sighed, "We knew that wasn't going to happen."

Stuart cleared his throat. Holly could tell something else was on his mind but she didn't say anything. She simply waited for him to spit it out. "Are you still leaving him?" he asked, with a slight stutter and certain amount of awkwardness.

2.

Jack followed one of the islanders out to a car park which was little more than a mud clearing coated in volcanic rock and dust. There were a few cars parked up, at all angles. The islander - dressed in a smart-looking uniform showcasing the brand of the resort - led him towards a four-by-four, jangling keys as he took each stride. As they neared the jeep, he tossed the keys to Jack who was more excited than strictly necessary.

"You treat her well," the islander whispered in broken English. "She pride and joy." Jack wasn't sure whether they were looking at the same vehicle. Pride and joy? He couldn't have been talking about the jeep in front of him. It didn't have a straight panel on the whole body and was covered in both dirt and deep scratches to the already-shoddy paintwork. Still, a deal was a deal. Jack reached into his pocket and pulled out a bundle of notes. He handed it to the islander who greedily started counting. "Need petrol," the islander said as he stuffed the monetary notes into his back pocket.

"I just gave you a fuck-ton of money and you didn't even ensure it was full?"

The islander looked at him as though he was speaking another language which, to him, he was. Jack shook his head, "Where do I get fuel?" he asked.

The islander laughed, "Petrol station! Funny man!" He walked away, shaking his head in disbelief at the stupid question. Of course Jack knew to get fuel from the petrol station. He wasn't an imbecile, despite having paid over the odds for this clapped out piece of shit which, apparently, was running on empty, but that still didn't mean he had an idea of where the filling station was. He sighed heavily and climbed into the jeep after struggling to unlock it with the bent key. He was angry with himself for not checking the state of the vehicle before agreeing to the deal. He should have known better after noticing the way the worker's friends had been laughing as they shook hands. He'd been had. They both knew it.

"Don't stress… Gets you out of the fucking resort," Jack muttered to himself as he reached across the jeep and pulled a tatty map from the glove compartment. The jeep might have set him back most of his holiday allowance but at least the islander had permitted the use of the map for free. The way these people haggled, it wouldn't have surprised him had it cost extra. He spread the map out over the bonnet of the jeep and started to study it when - from behind him - he heard the sounds of laughter. He didn't turn around. He didn't need to. It was Holly, Corinna, and Stuart. They'd seen the jeep then.

"Nice. And how much did you pay to borrow this?" Stuart teased.

"Fuck off."

"What's the score then? Do you get charged extra if you bring it back with a straight panel?"

"Seriously, mate, what did you expect out here? A Bentley? This place is poor as fuck. We should be thankful one of them even had a jeep that they were willing to lend us."

"Is this even safe to travel in?" Corinna asked. She had noticed the near bald tyres; not just one or two but all four.

"It's sound," Jack said, his mood not being helped by their negativity. Why couldn't they just be happy to get out of the resort for a while? He knew they couldn't have been as happy as they pretended to be there. It was fucking boring. Stuart, at least…

Stuart would have been bored there. People like Stuart and Jack, they weren't made out for places like this. It wasn't in their blood. They needed adventure. They needed something to do which didn't involve sitting in the sun and slowly developing the distinct possibility of skin cancer.

Stuart stood next Jack and looked at the map alongside him, "Where are we headed then?" Despite being annoyed at Stuart's earlier teasing, Jack pointed to the map. A small beach to the East of the largest volcano on the island. "We're going there?"

"That's right."

"And you reckon white sands?"

"That's what he said."

"Is that before or after he made it clear he was going to rip you off for borrowing his death-trap of a car? There's no way there is going to be white sand there. Look!" he tapped down on the page, where the mountain was. "That's the fucking volcano. I'm telling you... If there's sand there at all, it will be black as ash."

"He said..."

"Did he tell you he had a nice jeep to borrow?"

"He said he had a vehicle I could rent."

"Did he describe it with the word nice at any point?"

"I don't know. I can't remember."

"Black sand. I'm telling you..."

"Let's just go and take a look, yeah? And when you see it's white sand, you can apologise to me."

"Fine. Okay. But it will be black," Stuart climbed into the front as the two girls had already claimed a space each in the rear. Jack messily folded the map back up again and jumped into the driver's seat. He fiddled with the key until he managed to get it into the ignition. Carefully, fearful that it might snap there and then, he turned it. The engine spluttered into life. "Least it works, I suppose." Stuart turned back to the girls and gave them a cheeky little wink as he continued winding Jack up about his great deal. "Excited to see some black sand, ladies?" The two girls stifled a laugh.

Jack ignored him and inadvertently gave him something else to mock, "Yeah well we need a petrol station first." Stuart turned to facing forward again and glanced at the needle on the dial. It was in the red. He couldn't help but laugh.

"Gets better and better," Stuart teased.

The battered jeep spluttered its way from the makeshift carpark and hacked its way up the narrow street, the only direction they could venture in without hitting the unusually choppy sea. In the rearview mirror, no one noticed the islander watching them drive off. His mobile phone, pressed between shoulder and ear as he used both hands to count the money Jack had given him.

In the jeep, Stuart leaned down to the radio and turned it on. There was nothing but the crackling sound of static broadcasting over the airways. He started fiddling with the dial in an attempt to pick up a station. "Mate," he complained, "not even the radio works. He saw you coming a mile off." He started to laugh, "I bet you don't even have enough fuel to get to the petrol station. You paid all that money to get out and push us there."

"If anyone is going to be doing the pushing, it's you!" Jack flashed him a look. He didn't mind the odd bit of teasing but Stuart needed to back off now. Enough was enough. Especially given the fact that Jack already felt as though he'd been ripped off. He didn't need someone rubbing it in his face even more. Stuart stifled his laughter and looked out of the passenger window. He'd give him a couple of minute's peace and then he'd start again.

"So what's with the need for the constant buzz of adrenaline?" Corinna asked from the back. She was looking at Jack via the reflection of the rearview mirror. He kept one eye on the road as he spoke to her.

"What are you talking about?" he asked. "I don't constantly need to feel adrenaline. This beach - this is about paradise, right? This is about getting away from the built-up tourist areas and seeing the bits they don't like us seeing…"

"Aren't you the one who usually chooses the holidays which involve doing something stupid, or dangerous?"

"What? Like what?"

"Skiing?" Corinna replied instantly.

Jack felt his face redden a little. He enjoyed skiing. Both Jack and Stuart had gone every year before their relationships had come along. He had just wanted to share that passion with the woman he loved. What had happened on that slope - to him - was an unfortunate accident. He thought she was okay. She was going steadily and seemed to have control over what she was doing. It was an accident. Something he told himself again, and again, over the weeks which followed. To Holly, and Stuart, it was a sign he'd abandoned Holly. He had left her to please himself. But then, they were just looking for any excuse to drive a wedge in that relationship as they fought with their feelings for one another.

"That's not exactly adrenaline," Jack argued. "It's just a little more active than a beach holiday. These are all very well and nice but - and you have to feel the same - it can get a little dull sitting on the same sun-lounger for a week."

Corinna shook her head, "Not if you have your kindle and a selection of good books."

"Reading is boring. I'd rather do something…"

"So you admit you're an adrenaline junkie?"

"What? No. But books? Come on…"

"Books can take you to another place. They can take you on an adventure. If you really invest into it and let yourself go… You can feel what the characters feel."

"What if they're being tortured? What if you're reading some book like, I don't know… Something over the top… Some sick bastard's thing with loads of cannibalism and rape… You want to feel that?"

"Some readers do. That's the nice thing about books though, there is something for everyone. People who want to get transported to a world of torture porn can be; people seeking romance can find the stories that appeal to them… Or adventure… Or even erotica…"

"If people need to get a buzz from reading erotica, there's something very wrong with their lives."

"Why?"

"Because they should just put the book down and fuck their partner…"

"It's not about that…"

Holly interrupted, "Give up, you won't change his mind or convert him into being a book reader. The last thing he read was a copy of The Beano." She sounded genuinely disappointed, "Hell, even if he is watching a film… If there hasn't been an explosion within the first five minutes or a hint of nudity or gun play - he tends to fall asleep."

"Because he's an adrenaline junkie," Corinna laughed.

"I'm not!" he argued again.

"Okay, then it's because you have the mentality of a four year old," Corinna smiled at him.

Jack went to argue further with her but stopped when Stuart pointed ahead of them, "Over there." He'd spotted a petrol station on the horizon. "Least you won't have to push us now," he said.

"Fuck you," he said - a response which successfully answered both Corinna and Stuart.

#

The petrol station was a single man affair. One solitary pump, controlled by the man who may or may not have owned the station, and a tiny little shop which seemed to have more dust and crap than actual product. Despite having only just jumped into the jeep, all of the passengers took the opportunity to stretch their legs. Holly accompanied Jack into the store to pay and Corinna and Stuart were standing by the unusually quiet roadside. Stuart was watching a donkey across the road. A strange sight to behold considering the animal was just tethered to a small wooden stake in an open space of dirt and dust - much like the carpark they'd not long since left.

"Do you think it's the owner's ride?" Stuart mused. "Can't afford to buy a car so he uses a little donkey instead?" None of the people local to the immediate area seemed to carry much weight on their bodies so it wouldn't have been much of a hardship for a donkey to carry one of them. But why else would the donkey be standing there, tied to the pole?

"Did you sleep on the sofa all night?" Corinna had woken in the morning to find Stuart sprawled out across the sofa at an angle which couldn't have been comfortable. He was fully dressed, with a small sheet - pulled from the cupboard - draped over himself.

"I got in quite late and you were spread-eagled in the bed. I didn't want to wake you," he said. "You looked so peaceful."

She smiled at him, "I wouldn't have minded." She put her arm around him and cuddled in close to his side. He concentrated on the donkey, seemingly uninterested in putting his arm around her. She hadn't been taking up most of the bed last night. He simply felt as though it would have been two-faced to get into bed with her after the frank conversation he'd had with Holly the previous night. Despite what he said, and what he was looking at now, his mind wasn't on the donkey. His mind was on getting home, back to England. The thought of Holly having that conversation with Jack and him telling Corinna that he couldn't be with her anymore. Conversations he was part dreading and part looking forward to.

"For you!" Inside the petrol station - if you could call it that - the attendant was trying to pass a strange model of the island's volcano over to Holly. "Take!"

Holly took it and thanked the man, "How much is it?" she asked. She didn't even want it but felt it rude to refuse him when he was being so pushy about her taking it. It wasn't exactly an attractive ornament; a cheap looking pewter material.

"For you? Free!" he said. "Pretty lady!"

Holly felt her face flush, "Thank you." Now she really couldn't refuse it. She held it up for closer inspection, had it not been for the fact the attendant had told her it was a statue of the volcano, she wouldn't have even known. She would have simply presumed it to be a weird shaped rock; one of many the quaint little store seemed to stock when she saw the whole back wall behind the counter was filled with them.

"Nothing for me?" Jack asked, half-joking and half-serious.

"For ladies only," the attendant said as he rung the petrol through the dated till. He held his hand out for payment, which Jack duly handed over.

"Seems a bit sexist," Jack complained as he took his change. He dropped it into his back pocket and walked from the store; pulling the door open and causing the little bell above it to sing out. Holly thanked the attendant and followed Jack, still embarrassed she'd been given - for all intents and purposes - a gift.

Jack called Stuart and Corinna over as he jumped into the front of the jeep. They left the donkey and joined their friends in the vehicle.

"What the hell is that?" Corinna laughed when she saw the strange model.

"Don't ask."

As the jeep pulled away from the rusty pump, the attendant walked from his shop. With a machete in hand, he crossed the road to the now-anxious donkey. A low rumble of thunder ripped through the otherwise clear sky as the attendant raised the blade high in the air. The donkey started to back away from him - not that the rope tying it to the stake permitted it much movement. The blade came down as the jeep disappeared around a corner.

#

"Do you know where you're going?" Stuart asked Jack as the two girls quietly nattered in the back; various conversations about this and that - none of which was interesting enough for Stuart to warrant joining in. They'd been driving for nearly thirty minutes now and it had dawned on Stuart that the only time Jack had checked the map was when they were back at the resort.

"It looked like a straight line from point A through to B," Jack said. He wasn't irritated anymore. The soothing drive along the near deserted road had beaten the stress from him. Had he been driving through the rammed streets of London, back home, it could have been a different story. "Looked pretty straight forward, besides…" Stuart cringed; he knew what was coming. "Harder to have an adventure if you don't get lost once in a while," he finished. Stuart had lost count of the number of times he'd heard that saying and, each time, it made him want to hit Jack. Unaware, Jack continued, "You can't say this isn't nice, right? Us, windows wound down, wind blowing through, the open roads… It's great!"

Corinna looked at Holly. The pair had just been talking about how much they loved the sun-loungers and soaking up the sun with a glass of white wine each - and a bottle of water close to hand for when the sun got too much. A good book for company. They both, rightly so, bit their tongues. One day for Jack to have his 'adventure' and then the holiday was back to what they both craved; rest and relaxation.

"Anyone else think that is strange?" Stuart asked. He was referring to another small rumble of thunder. The skies were brilliant blue with not a cloud in sight, not even a faint wisp in the distance. Yet, once again, there was the familiar sound of thunder. Nothing major, just a low tremor as though a storm were being threatened. "Don't you need to have clouds for thunder?"

"I don't think so," said Jack. "It's just high pressure meeting low pressure, isn't it?" Neither really knew what they were talking about. All Stuart knew was that he'd never heard the rumblings of thunder without at least one flash of lightning and some form of cloud cover. Having a perfect day, blisteringly hot, yet still hearing thunder was strange to him. "Did you know Stuart was scared of thunder?" Jack looked to Corinna via the rearview mirror. "You might have to let Holly sit up here so he can hold your hand."

"I didn't say I was scared. I just found it strange," Jack replied. He was still looking up at the sky to see if he could see any sign of a storm approaching. There was nothing. Even the top of the mountains which lined the horizon in the distance, appeared to have perfectly clear skies around the summits. "It is kind of creepy though. Like something from an episode of The Twilight Zone."

"You're just confused because it's always raining in England," Holly said. He turned to her and she smiled.

"Nah, he's just a pussy!" Jack laughed.

Stuart sighed; it was his turn to be teased then.

"It's just unusual," he said. "Normally thunder is accompanied with rain and lightning."

"Not all the time," Corinna laughed.

"Okay, forget I said anything."

She laughed harder, "Are you seriously sulking now? Oh, baby!" She let out of a scream as Jack yanked on the steering wheel and took the jeep off-road, onto a tiny dirt trail. "What are you doing?"

He laughed, "Sorry, nearly missed the turn off."

The road went from serviceable concrete to mud and loose stones, surrounded by dry patches of wasteland covered in fine sand and a thin layer of dust. The passengers bounced around as the jeep pounded the uneven surface.

"You mind slowing down a little?" Holly shouted from the back as she put her hands on the seat in front of her in an effort to steady herself. Jack responded with a laugh and put his foot down so that it was flat against the floor. The back tires kicked up a cloud of dirt as the jeep tore off towards the coastline; the back end of the vehicle sliding out slightly until Jack managed to pull it back in with a little opposite lock of the steering wheel. Both of the girls screamed as Jack and Stuart cheered.

"Fucking adrenaline-junkie! I told you!" Corinna shouted from the back. She too was clutching the seat in front of her own.

3.

The jeep was parked up at an angle. Stopped from going further by large rocks which were seemingly dotted around the landscape, right up to the beginning of the thick jungle at the base of the mountain range. On the other side of the rocks, the sea gently lapped away at the beach's sandy shores. Black sand.

"So… These pure white beaches then?" Corinna enjoyed teasing Jack. She liked the fact it was easy to get a reaction from him. He was standing on one of the rocks, looking into the distance to see if he could see a point where black turned white. He couldn't. He jumped down from the rock and walked towards where the dirt turned to sand. Corinna shook her head in the disbelief she wasn't even worth an answer. Stuart followed Jack in a bid to keep the peace. He knew what Jack was like if he didn't get something he was expecting; a little like a petulant child.

"Maybe it's further round?" he suggested.

"The guy is a cunt. He conned me," Jack moaned as he stepped his sandalled foot onto the fine black sand. "I paid a fucking fortune to borrow his jeep for this. It looks exactly the same as the last fucking beach we were at!"

"Well…" Stuart sought out the positive, "There are no sun-loungers or screaming children." The lack of screaming children was one positive at least. The resort's beach did have a habit of getting noisy during the day whether it be the sound of screaming children or excited children.

"I'm going to get my money back when I see him. Either that or I'll trash the jeep," Jack continued his rant. Stuart turned back to the bent and battered vehicle. He was unsure how you could possibly make it look any worse than the way it looked at the moment. "Takes the piss. Just because we're foreign, they think they can take us for a bunch of mugs."

"Look, we're here now - we may as well enjoy it." Stuart turned to call the girls over to join them but realised they weren't even looking at them. They were staring in the opposite direction, their eyes transfixed by something beyond the rocks and unseen by Stuart. "What's up with them?" he asked. "I'll be back in a minute," he said as he headed off to fetch them.

When he neared them he realised they were looking towards the tree lines. A young lad was standing there watching them. Black hair, black eyes, tanned skin, and dressed in nothing but some kind of loin cloth which looked to be made from animal hide of some description. The two girls were waving at him, even trying to coax him over, but the boy did nothing but stare.

"I didn't realise they had tribes here," Holly whispered to Stuart as his eyes were also drawn to the boy. As soon as he wasn't hidden by the row of rocks, the boy spotted Stuart and ran back into the dense trees, disappearing from sight. "You scared him off!" Holly laughed.

"He was clearly afraid of my strong physique," Stuart laughed. "Come on, we need to get down to the beach, Jack is having a paddy down there."

"Oh no! Quick! Let's go and make sure he is okay. Does he want a hug? Should I offer him a 'feel better' hand-job?" the sarcasm oozed from Corinna's voice. She caught herself doing it and apologised to Holly. Jack was, after all, her boyfriend and she must have loved him.

"Don't apologise," Holly laughed as she made her way towards her lost looking boyfriend, "it would save me from having to do it later."

Corinna laughed and, taking Stuart's hand, followed on. With Holly a good few steps ahead, Corinna whispered to Stuart, "Does Jack always get his own way?"

"Pretty much. Most of the holidays we go on are his idea but - to be honest - he is the one who organises them so, you know… Only reason we're on this one is because he felt guilty about what happened at the ski resort and felt duty bound to give Holly a proper holiday."

Corinna stopped Stuart from walking and cuddled into him, "Well I'm happy we're here even if I think your friend is an idiot." She looked out to the sparkling sea, the reflection of the sunshine dancing beautifully across the top of the waves. It was romantic. For her at least. For Stuart, it was the beginning of the end. The good weather and free-flowing drinks were enough to make him realise, and Holly too, that they were with the wrong people. He yearned to hold Holly's hand, walking down the stretch of sand (golden or black, he wasn't fussed), not Corinna's. He kept telling himself, only a few more days and they'd both be breaking up with their partners. They could both be together.

A low rumble in the sky.

"At least it's quiet!" Holly said as she reached Jack. He was standing close to the sea, skimming a few rocks found on the beach into the water with little to no success.

"It's a shit-hole. Just like the last beach back at the resort. The difference is I spent a fucking fortune getting us here."

"Relax. It's nice. Look, you have the forest around the mountains, there are no children running around annoying us… It's lovely." She waited for Jack to throw the next stone and then she moved up to him and put her arms around him. He sighed and put one arm around her. "And there's a tribe nearby."

"What?"

She laughed, "We were looking at the trees and there was this kid just standing there watching us! Jack scared him back into the forest but - yeah - wouldn't have seen that back at the resort so that's something too. A real tribesman. Well, child... But close enough." Jack perked up. Still in his embrace with Holly, he turned his head to the forests. "What is it?" Holly asked. She immediately realised she'd said the wrong thing. Any hint of the possibility of seeing something different was enough to pique Jack's interest and get him on a mission to hunt it out. He'd once taken them on a two week camping trip to Scotland because he had a whim to see the Loch Ness Monster for himself. Obviously it didn't happen. They saw rain, they saw gnats, they came home.

"Which way did he go?" Jack asked.

"He's long gone now I expect. Should have seen the speed with which he disappeared. Never seen anyone move so fast but then... He did see Stuart's face. That would be enough to scare anyone."

"Which way?" Jack asked again.

"I don't remember."

Jack pulled away from Holly's embrace and started up the beach towards the trees. She sighed and started to follow, passing Corinna and Stuart as she did.

"Now what?" Corinna asked.

"I accidentally mentioned the kid."

Stuart sighed; a long suffering sigh too. He knew it meant they were about to head out on some kind of jungle expedition whether they liked it or not. By the time Corinna cottoned on to what was going on, Jack was already in the forest.

"We're going in there?" she asked. Her eyes were wide with not fear but rather concern. Here they were, on an island they knew very little about - heading off into what looked to be a thick jungle. "Do you know much about tribes because I don't... What if they're like overprotective farmers? You know, chasing people off their land with shotguns? Or - in this case - long, pointy sticks? And do we even know what is in that forest? I mean, animals?" Corinna didn't have much of a choice but to get dragged along with the others, despite her protests. She wasn't about to hang around by herself even though she had no wish to venture into the woods. "I just want to go on record now to say I believe this is a really, really bad idea."

"It'll be fine," Stuart said as they neared the tree-line. "He'll get bored and turn around. He always does."

"Unless he finds something," Holly helpfully pointed out.

Jack was standing in a small clearing within the dense woodlands. He was looking from side to side for any hint of a tribe, or lost child.

"Which way did he go?" he asked again as the rest of the group reached him.

"He disappeared. We didn't see."

"Let's go," Corinna moaned again, hoping that - for once - Jack would stop and listen to what someone else wanted to do.

"Come on," Jack pushed, "this is cool. Don't you want to find a lost tribe?"

"I doubt they're lost. It's not like these woods are similar in size to the Amazon. Besides," Stuart continued, "it was probably just some kid on a day out with his mum and dad. Who knows what they wear out here..."

Jack ignored Stuart and started walking up the slight gradient to what appeared to be another clearing through the next thicket of trees.

"Really?" Corinna moaned once more.

"You guys have got to see this!" Jack called down to them as he passed through the thicket. One by one they sighed as they followed in his footsteps; none of them exactly excited to be doing so. As they reached him they noticed he was standing by a large tree which seemingly stretched for a mile or so into the sky. It was a tall tree - yes - but hardly anything to get excited about.

"What is it?" Holly asked.

"Look!" Jack pointed up the tree, about a quarter ways. There, sticking from the side of it, was what appeared to be an arrow. "There is a tribe round here!" he said. The tone in his voice suggesting he was like an excited schoolboy or famous explorer who'd discovered some ancient, lost civilisation.

"You see, that doesn't make me want to find them any sooner. It's an arrow… A weapon… It makes me want to get out of here," Corinna said. Her irritation was growing.

"Relax," Jack laughed at her, "they were probably out hunting."

"Hunting what exactly? We know nothing about this place or the animals that live here. We shouldn't be in here!" Corinna felt her rage growing more and more by the second. Even her fist had clenched into a tight ball which she desperately wanted to throw Jack's way.

"Maybe she's right," Holly said. She too felt uneasy about being in the trees. Her mind thinking more about the animals living within than the possibility of a tribe being there. Were there poisonous snakes? Spiders? Wild cats? Her mind answered yes to all animals feared and every time she heard a branch snap, or a bush rustle… it was one of them coming to get her.

Jack turned to Stuart, "Give me a bunk up?" He walked over to the tree and put his arms around its wide base. He then gripped the trunk tightly with his legs too. In his head it was a simple act, to shuffle his way up the tree, but in reality - he was going nowhere fast. He just looked retarded. Stuart couldn't help but to laugh, "I'm not sure that's the best way of doing it," he said. It didn't take Jack long to realise that he was probably right and he released the tree.

"Give me a bunk up then!" He waited by the tree. Stuart interlocked his fingers and bent down a little, placing his hands on his knee for added support. Jack stepped up onto his hands and placed one of his own hands on Stuart's shoulder and the other against the tree. The girls took a step back. "Ready?" Jack asked. Stuart nodded and braced himself as Jack put his whole weight down onto Stuart's hands and knee. Both men grunted, one as he took the weight of his friend and the other as he reached up for the arrow sticking from the tree's thick trunk. The grunts of both men disguised the whooshing sound splicing through the air. The strained grunting of Stuart drowned out the gargled noise from Jack's throat as a second arrow pierced his back, ripping through the front of his chest and into the tree, close to where the first arrow was still wedged. Jack's body went limp as the initial shock took all coordination from him. His arms dropped to his sides. He screamed out as did the two girls when they realised what had happened. A second scream from both as they turned and saw an elderly man standing back down towards where they'd first entered the woods, a bow in one hand, an arrow in the other. Stuart fell away from Jack, landing on his back. He raised his hands to protect himself from being squashed as his friend's body fell back down upon him but it didn't come. He slowly lowered his hands when he realised that Jack was pinned to the tree, screaming. His legs were just hanging there, swaying helplessly as he tried to take some of the weight of his own body by embracing the tree trunk. Stuart spun onto his front, then all fours and then up to his feet - just in time to see the tribesman loading a second arrow into the long bow.

"Run!" Stuart screamed to the girls as he pushed them towards the thicket. "Don't look back! Just fucking run!" He was first through, breaking the foliage down with his hands raised as he hurried through. The two girls, close behind him. Jack screamed from the tree, begging them not to leave him. For their own safety, it was a scream ignored.

A second arrow fired through the air and tore into Jack's back. That too pierced through to the front of his chest and bedded itself into the tree. The hunter smiled as Jack screamed out again.

"Fuck you!" he yelled as the tribesman walked over to the tree, sliding the bow over his right shoulder. "Fuck you!" Jack repeated. He couldn't see the man who'd fired the bolts. He could just hear him; the sound of his footsteps, the sound of his laugh, and then a muttered sentence in a language he didn't recognise. "FUCK YOU!"

#

Jack was sitting by Holly's hospital bed. Her leg was in plaster, lifted from the bed on a support system. By the side of her bed was a trolley with an uneaten dinner on it and, next to the plate, a cup of water with a small medicine cap containing two circular pills. Jack looked sheepish. He felt as though he were to blame for what happened despite it being an accident. He had pushed Holly to come down the bigger of the mountains with him. Not just that, he'd then left her to come down alone so he could try and beat his quickest time. He should have stayed with her. Easy to think that in hindsight though after something had gone wrong. Had nothing happened, the chances were he would be back up that mountain doing the same thing again and again, leaving her to play catch up or sit out and watch.

"How are you feeling?" he asked.

Holly wasn't really feeling anything. The strong medication saw to that. At least, with regards to the pain she was in anyway. She still felt disappointment that her partner had left her and not been there when she needed him. Another nail in the coffin of their relationship, which she was pretty sure he knew nothing about. As far as he was concerned, their relationship didn't even have a coffin yet, let alone nails in it.

Jack hadn't apologised for what had happened. It's not that he didn't feel as though an apology was due. It was more to the point that he didn't know how to say it. He had left her. Had he stayed with her, maybe she wouldn't have even taken the tumble? Maybe they'd both still be up there, on the mountain, having fun or, maybe, they'd be relaxing in the cabin's hot tub? A few drinks, celebrating a fun, eventful day?

"They said you could leave in the morning. They just want to keep an eye on you overnight," he continued. One night to make sure she didn't suffer from the hit she'd sustained on her head. She'd told them she hadn't lost consciousness but it didn't matter. They still wanted to keep her in for the night. Of course she already knew this. She didn't need Jack telling her. They'd told her themselves when they last did the rounds before dinner was brought around. "I asked if there was any way I could stay with you but they said no. Said the rest would do you some good," he continued filling in the void of silence. "But I can come back early in the morning to take you home." He paused a moment, "Just need to figure out how. Get some transportation, or something, I guess." His tone was completely wrong for the moment. It did nothing to make her feel good about him coming to collect her in the morning and, instead, made her feel as though she were an inconvenience.

"Sorry to be such an inconvenience," she said. He looked her in the eye and saw that he'd chosen the wrong words.

"You're not," he said - correcting himself. "I just meant I'm not sure who to ask for that sort of thing…" The ski-resort he had chosen was close to the airport. There were transfers from airport to resort via a free shuttle bus. They had had no reason to hire a car and - even if they had - none of them particularly wanted to drive in the snow, even though most of the main roads were heavily treated to protect from snow and ice. "We could get a taxi," he said. "I can arrange that."

"That's good of you," Holly said sarcastically.

He cleared his throat and asked the question he already knew the answer to, "Are you mad at me?"

Holly started to laugh. For the briefest of seconds, Jack wondered whether it was something to do with the medication she'd been drip-fed. "Why would I be mad at you?" she asked. It was a rhetorical question, one which Jack thankfully recognised. "I told you I didn't want to come on this holiday. I told you what I wanted - beaches, sun, sea, relaxation - but, no, you had to go ahead and book this. I told you I couldn't ski very well. You had to drag me up that mountain. And then, if that wasn't enough, you left me. And you haven't even said sorry for doing so. You haven't even apologised for leaving me there, in the snow, with a broken leg. I was alone. I was scared and where were you? Racing down the mountain to try and beat some pathetic time. But no, of course I'm not mad at you. Why would I be?"

Jack shifted in his seat as a feeling of guilt washed over him. Without much thought he blurted out, "I'm sorry."

"I don't want you to say it because you feel duty bound to," Holly immediately picked him up. "I want you to say it because you mean it!"

"I do mean it. I'm sorry. I didn't think. I am genuinely sorry. If I could turn the clock back, I would. I feel like a piece of shit that I wasn't there for you but I am now. And I'm not going anywhere."

"It's never you is it," Holly said.

"What do you mean?"

"That gets hurt," she finished. "It's never you that gets hurt. It's always someone else and it's always because of one of your hair-brained ideas…" The words hit home. It wasn't the first time someone had gotten hurt because of something Jack had organised. This broken leg was just another situation in a string of incidences. Holly was right; it was never Jack who got hurt. It was always someone else. "One day you won't be so lucky," she warned him. "One day you'll get yourself in trouble and - I hope - when that day comes, you're alone…"

4.

Jack screamed out as the hunter pulled him down from the tree with a sharp tug. His scream echoed through the woods as he landed hard on the forest floor. He slumped to his side, still with the two arrows sticking through his body. The stranger was talking to him. His tongue rapidly clicking in his mouth. Saliva shooting from between his lips, hitting Jack in the face. He suddenly stopped speaking and took a hold of the arrow closest to his hand. He smiled as he gave it a shake from side to side, tearing Jack's insides a little more in the process.

"Fuck you!" Jack screamed when he was finally able to form words as opposed to pained sounds.

"Fuck…you. Fuck…you…. Fuck you…" the hunter repeated. He twisted the arrow in a counter-clockwise direction, causing Jack to scream again. Another smile spread across the man's foul mouth as - without warning - he ripped the arrow out in a hard tug away from the chest. Jack screamed out loud as the man laughed and tore out the second arrow, dropping them both to the ground. The stranger leaned down and stroked Jack's cheek with the palm of his hand. As he did so he looked Jack straight in the eye and quietly shushed him, as though comforting him. Jack fought back the tears as he tried his damnedest to relax despite the situation he had found himself in. Swearing hadn't worked for him and the more wound up he was, the faster the blood would flow. The man said something else to him; another flurry of random noises and clicks of the tongue. His face, inches from Jacks.

Jack could smell the man's rotten breath and tried desperately hard not to gag. Teeth missing and those which were present were blackened with rot. "Please don't hurt me," Jack pleaded, despite knowing the man didn't understand a word he was saying. Or so he presumed at least. He repeated himself again, "Please don't hurt me."

The hunter grabbed Jack by the shoulder and manoeuvred him around so that he was on his back. Blood leaking from his back wounds onto the muddy ground, blood seeping from the front - staining his top. Jack couldn't help but let out another yelp of pain as the man knelt down on his chest. His full weight, both knees, making it hard to breathe. He leaned down to Jack's face once more. That stinking breath. Jack tried to ask him to get off but the words only came out as a strained wheeze as he struggled for oxygen.

Something else was said, from man to man. Something else that was lost on foreign ears. Jack started to cry as the man's face got closer and closer to his own. Tears spilled from a combination of both fear and pain. The hunter pushed Jack's head to the side. He opened his mouth and carefully closed it around Jack's ear. Jack struggled fruitlessly under the man's weight as he felt his ear fold in half inside the stranger's mouth; his teeth pushing down on both top and bottom until the two tips touched. Jack froze, too afraid to move. He could feel the man's breath in his hair, just above his ear, from where he was breathing through his nose. But harder to ignore was the native's tongue running over his twisted ear.

Jack's face started to turn blue as he became more and more frantic for oxygen. A brief reprieve as the tribesman lifted his weight slowly allowing Jack the opportunity to take in another lungful of the humid air. A short lived reprieve as the hunter put his weight back down upon the terrified youth before finally biting down hard and clamping his teeth together. Jack's scream echoed through the dense woodlands as the tribesman pulled away from Jack's head with a twist of his own neck; the ear gripped between his teeth with blood dripping from it. He tilted his head back and let it greedily slip into his mouth where he started rolling it around with his tongue, savouring the full flavour as Jack continued to scream out for his friends to come and help him. The hunter's lips smacked together as he started to chew noisily; the sound of the ear ripping apart into smaller pieces as he crunched it's squidgy flesh down making it easier to swallow bites. He gulped it down before twisting Jack's head to a forward facing position.

"It's never you that gets hurt. It's always someone else and it's always because of one of your hair-brained ideas... One day you won't be so lucky. One day you'll get yourself in trouble and - I hope - when that day comes, you're alone..." Holly's words, spoken in anger when she'd broken her leg, kept playing through his mind over and over, despite Jack's wish to block them out. He closed his eyes to the sight of the tribesman leaning upon him, smiling a bloody smile. Jack felt two thumbs press against both of his eyelids as the hunter forced him to open his eyes to see what was coming. He kept his thumbs there, refusing to release his lids, refusing to let him close his eyes once more. That smile. That damned smile, bloody and taunting.

"Fuck you!" Jack wheezed.

The tribesman grabbed Jack's face; fingers on one of his cheeks and thumb on the other. He pulled Jack's jaw down as he squeezed tightly, forcing the mouth into an open 'O' shape. Jack tried to speak out but couldn't as the hunter reached into his mouth with his dirty hand and took a hold of his tongue. Muffled moans of pain, anger, and fear came from Jack's mouth as he tried to struggle against the grip holding him still. What his words failed to convey, his eyes showed perfectly: a desperation for the man to release him. A hope that this was nothing but a prank; a bad dream at worst.

The hunter slowly pushed his fingers into Jack's open mouth. Digits with long nails, black caked underneath, gripped Jack's tongue and stopped it from flapping. Something spoken; clicks of the tongue. Another smile of bloody teeth stained with juice from the ear and then…

#

Holly's hands were over her ears and her eyes were scrunched tight closed. Just as her cruel words - back at the hospital - had played on Jack's mind, they were now playing on hers too. The first scream had made her want to cry out in answer. The only reason she hadn't was because of Stuart's hand clamped around her mouth as he held her tight and stopped her from screaming, fearful of giving away their position.

They were hiding in a bush, all three of them. And all three of them were petrified. Holly was sitting closest to the small opening in the foliage. Corinna was to her side and Stuart was behind them both having led the way. One of his hands being on Holly's mouth, to help keep her quiet, and one being on her shoulder for comfort; not that it was currently offering much.

They'd run as far as they could and Stuart had only forced them into the cramped hiding place when he was certain that they weren't being followed. At first he didn't understand why they'd been left to get away, not that they had anywhere to go but deeper into the forests due to the lay-out of the land and the fact the murderer had been between them and their getaway vehicle. It was only after he'd heard Jack's first pained scream that he realised why they hadn't been followed.

Holly pulled Stuart's shaking hand away from her mouth as tears streamed down her face. She wasn't the only one crying. Stuart was holding it together, despite being scared, but Corinna wasn't. She too was crying as the fear consumed her.

"We have to go back!" Holly said as soon as Stuart's hand was away from her mouth. She spoke in a hushed voice. They knew they were alone. They knew - at that particular moment - they were safe. It didn't mean they wanted to start shouting though.

"We can't."

Jack's muffled scream tore through the jungle and straight through their souls. It wasn't as loud as the first scream but Holly knew - they all did - that it wasn't because whatever was happening to him was hurting any less. She sobbed again and pleaded for the group to go back for him. She knew there was nothing they could do for him though. They all did. Jack roared out in pain again, a different sound to the last scream. Something had changed. Holly wept once more. It was one thing to want to leave someone, it was another to hear them being slowly tortured to death.

"We should keep moving," Corinna said. Her eyes wide, filled with fear, were watching the bushes across the path from their hiding place. She felt like a sitting duck there, hiding in the bush, and wanted to keep moving even though she had no idea where they were headed, other than deeper into the forest. "We can't just sit around and wait," she continued. Her whole body was visibly shaking. She couldn't dismiss the image of Jack pinned to the tree by the arrow in his back. In her mind, it was only a matter of time before the same thing happened to them too.

"We need to stay here," Stuart whispered.

The lay of the land meant they had only two directions to go in; one being back towards the hunter and the other deeper into the woodlands. Where they were now, opposite them heading back towards the beaches, was so thick with brambles and bushes that they'd not be able to get through quietly, and without getting themselves tangled. The last thing they needed was to be stuck in the vines with a murderer lining up an arrow on their trapped bodies. Not knowing the area, nor the wildlife within, Stuart didn't want to travel deeper into the forests yet, neither did he wish to head back towards the man with the bow and arrows who was clearly not afraid to use them.

"We can't just stay here!" Corinna said. Her fear and need to get away caused her voice to raise a little. Holly shushed her as she scanned the area, fearful someone would hear them. "They'll see us!" she panicked.

"There's no one coming. At the moment we're good. We go deeper and God only knows what we will find," Stuart said, keeping his voice low. "We wait here, we stick together, and then - when we think the coast is clear - we head back the way we came and try and sneak out of here."

"Back the way we came?"

"It's where the jeep is!" he tried to silence her again.

"It's also where the tribesman is!" Corinna argued, struggling to keep as quiet as Stuart.

"There was one. We saw one tribesman. How do you know there aren't more in that direction? It's our best bet. Just need to wait it out…"

"Until the coast is clear? And exactly when will you know the coast is clear?" she asked.

Jack screamed again. The three fell silent as they could do nothing but listen to their friend's cries. It was obvious to them all - now - that they knew the coast would be clear when Jack stopped screaming.

#

Blood spurted from Jack's mouth as the hunter jokingly flapped Jack's now-severed tongue around in his hand, taunting Jack who continued to try to cry out and weep. He watched helplessly as the tribesman held the tongue up to his own mouth and put it between his lips. He moved his hands away so the tongue just hung there as though a part of his open mouth. It slipped from between his lips when the man laughed again. Another hacking of blood as Jack's gag reflexes refused to swallow it down.

The tongue was collected from where it had landed on Jack's chest. The native held it back up to his own mouth and touched it with the tip of his own tongue. Jack wailed as best as he could considering he was missing his tongue and his mouth was permanently filling with gore. The sounds he was making - a mixture of grunts, screams and gargles - did nothing to deter the hunter from seemingly enjoying himself and he smiled at Jack before putting the tongue down upon his chest once more. Something else had caught his eye. Something even more appealing than the taste of tongue. Or rather, something with which to fold the tongue around; a fucked-up sandwich of human…

The man cocked his head to the side and leaned down close to Jack's face once more. His eyes fixed upon Jack's own, a look of fear and pain in Jack's eyes, a look of hunger in the hunter's. The tribesman licked his own thumb, along with the two nearest fingers before he pressed them against Jack's eye socket; the tips of the two fingers at the top of the socket and the tip of the thumb at the bottom. Clicks of his tongue as he said something, not that Jack heard. His mind was elsewhere. His mind was replaying another conversation.

Jack had been lying in bed next to Holly. They'd not long since started dating. At this time, their relationship was about a month old. Maybe less. They hadn't done anything but kiss. She was on her side, fully dressed, and he had been on his back with his head turned to her. He couldn't remember what they'd been talking about. The pain from his current situation making it hard to concentrate. Hard to remember. She was smiling. He remembered the smile. Whenever she smiled her whole face lit up. Her eyes seemed to brighten.

"Your eyes are amazing," he'd told her. She giggled. It had been the first real compliment he had given her without any expectation. He had told her she looked stunning on the first date, dressed in a little sexy red dress which clung to her figure perfectly, but that didn't count. Everyone does compliments on the first date. She'd told him that she liked his eyes too. The darkness. The depth. She said they made him look mysterious - whereas her own eyes made her look sweet and angelic, his words - not hers. The memory continued to play through. He'd leaned in close for a kiss, his hand on her hip.

The fingers dug into his skull and Jack couldn't help but gargle another shriek as they pushed in, past the eyeball. Jack winced as he felt the long digits curl around it, getting a grip. A peculiar feeling. An unpleasant sensation. He struggled under the man's weight once again but it didn't help move him or relieve the pressure felt at the back of the eye. Without any words, or sounds, the tribesman slowly started to pull the eye out of Jack's skull, causing yet more screaming from the distressed youth as the pain kicked in. Jack winced again as he felt the skin around the socket stretch to allow the eye to slide from within. His one good ear heard the 'pop' as it came away completely and he screamed another scream of pain as the hunter ripped it completely free so that he was just left with the eye in his bloody hand. In turn - Jack was left with a gaping hole. The hunter took the eye and placed it on the already-severed tongue before rolling it into a fucked up sausage roll. Clicks of his own tongue as he spoke to the still screaming Jack and then he took a bite. His teeth pierced the soft flesh of the tongue with ease but took a little more effort to burst through the eyeball, allowing the mixture of flavours into his mouth. He started chewing, letting more and more of the juices fill his mouth, mixing with his saliva and then - with a smile - he swallowed the first mouthful down. Blood mixed with flesh, mixed with the thin film of skin that had been on the outer edge of the eyeball. A burp. He continued to chew as Jack continued to scream; his one good eye watching the proceedings and unable to do a thing about it.

5.

The sun was beating down hard and the heat - especially the humidity - was starting to get to Stuart and the girls, despite the bush and trees offering some shade at least. With the exception of the occasional bird singing to a mate, somewhere in the distance, the woodlands had grown quiet. Jack had grown quiet.

Holly wiped a single tear from her cheek, with the back of her hand, as it spilled from her eye. Slowly she'd been coming to terms with what had happened. Slowly. She was still upset - and would be for a long, long time - but the tears had calmed a little. Corinna was in much the same state, although her tears had initially been more about losing her own life than the life of a man she didn't really like. All three were watching all around them for signs of movement within the bushes and trees. There was none.

A few more minutes slowly went by before Stuart crawled from the hide-y hole. Holly grabbed his arm as he neared the clearing.

"What are you doing?" she hissed.

"We can't stay here forever," he replied as he pulled himself free. He stood up tall in the middle of the clearing and stretched. His back clicked into place as he continued looking around. Despite how it could have looked to Holly and Corinna, he was scared. His eyes darted from bush to bush, taking in all of his surroundings, worried that - at any moment - an arrow was going to fly towards him.

There was a small temptation to call out to anyone in the near vicinity. Whilst he didn't want to make them aware of his presence, neither did he want them suddenly catching him by surprise. At least if he called out they'd answer and he'd know they were there. He refrained from saying anything. He just stood there, silent. Watching. Waiting. The girls didn't move. They stayed hidden in the bush, also watching. Their hearts beating hard in the back of their throats. They too were expecting a sudden arrow to slice the air, just as had happened to Jack. Stuart turned back to them and waved them from their hiding place. They both hesitated a moment, still unsure if it really was as safe as it seemed to be. Holly was first to crawl out on her hands and knees. Corinna was close behind.

"We have a choice," Stuart said, "we can either go back the way we came and hope they've gone or we can carry on into the woods and hope we find another clear path down to the beach? We're in this together so it has to be a joint decision." They all stood there a moment, neither one of them wishing to commit to something which could lead the others into trouble. "I'm going to need an answer. I can't make the decision for us… It needs to be a group thing."

Corinna looked back over her shoulder, deeper into the woods. She looked forward again towards the direction they'd come. "I can't hear anyone. Maybe it's okay to leave?" she said.

Stuart nodded and looked at Holly, "I feel the same. We know what is in that direction. We have no idea what we're running towards if we keep going deeper."

Holly nodded, "Okay."

"Okay? You're happy to go back the way we came?" he asked. She nodded again. "Okay well follow me then. We'll move quickly and quietly. Single file so if they are there - you two have a shot of getting away again. If anything happens just keep running in the opposite direction, okay? Don't try and help me. Just run." He was fully aware the chances of the girls stopping to help him were slim. It wasn't as though any of them had stopped for Jack but it didn't matter. He still believed it needed to be said. If anything it would give them some peace of mind should they get out and he didn't. He had told them to leave him. He had said to do it. It had been his idea. They were just doing what they were told.

Quietly, in single file, the trio crept back the way they had come. Each of them being careful to avoid treading on large sticks or twigs which may snap, causing unnecessary noise. Stuart upfront, Corinna behind him and Holly at the rear; each one holding the other for moral support. Each one hoping they didn't bump into the man with the bow and arrow.

Holly's mind kept circling back to when she and Jack had chosen to go to a theme park for the day. The sun had been shining - after a week of crap weather - and it had been a spur of the moment decision. Pack the car and head up the motorway for an hour and a half until they got to the theme park entrance. That was, after a quick stop-off on route at the local supermarket. Holly had remembered seeing vouchers on the side of some cornflake boxes offering the opportunity to purchase one ticket and get the second free. It would have been rude not to check to see if the vouchers were still on the packaging.

Although they had been fairly new into their relationship at this point, and Holly had wanted it to be just a day for them, Stuart had asked if he could tag along. Holly didn't have a say in it. Jack agreed stating the more the merrier. She didn't mind but - at the time - Stuart didn't have a partner so it meant traveling up as a threesome. Two's company, three's a crowd. The day had been pretty fun, despite her initial concerns she'd be playing gooseberry. As it was, Stuart was more than happy to venture off and do his own thing. He had just wanted a lift. When they went on a ride together, he'd be the one to offer to ride solo. And some of the rides permitted them to sit together anyway, or go in as a threesome at least. The Haunted House had been one such experience; a large maze of many corridors which were filled with live actors whose sole purpose was to scare the wandering groups of visitors.

"I'm not going first," Holly had told them. The boys tried to make her go in, leading the way, because they thought it would be more funny for them when the ghouls and ghosts, or whatever else was hiding within, leapt out at her. She would be the one on the firing line for all of the scares whilst they got to sit back and laugh at her expense. They must have argued for a good couple of minutes before she forced them in first. She, herself, took up the back without giving it much thought. Yes the person at the front of the chain, snaking its way through the maze, was often first to be pounced upon but it didn't mean the person at the back was safe. Sometimes one of the actors waited until they'd all entered the room and then they'd make their presence known by leaping out and grabbing the last person through. It was this scenario that was playing through Holly's mind now, as she kept looking back over her shoulder to ensure there was no one creeping up behind her. She hadn't meant to be at the back of the queue. Before she realised what was going on, Corinna had already claimed her position - the safest one - in the centre of the trio.

Holly broke the formation and stepped out front so that she was side by side with Stuart. Not wishing to be left behind, Corinna pushed her way between the two - keeping her position in the middle of the group.

"What are you doing?" Stuart asked.

"I don't want to be at the back," Holly replied. Clearly Stuart didn't remember what had happened back at the theme park. Hardly surprising when he had bigger concerns on his mind.

"We agreed it was the safest way to go…" Stuart started to argue with her.

"I don't want to go at the back," she interrupted. The tone in her voice made it very clear that her sudden change of heart wasn't up for discussion or negotiation. In her eyes she figured she'd be better off if they all walked in a line together, side by side. If anyone was going to come for them they could just scatter without fear of one falling back on the other. It also meant it was easier for them all to keep an eye open, especially if they occasionally checked behind them too. The group fell silent as they slowly made their way back in the direction they'd come from, each of them still being careful not to step on a branch, or anything else which would make unnecessary noise, each of them worried that their quickened heartbeats would be loud enough to be heard.

Corinna reached up and grabbed both Stuart and Holly by their arms, stopping them from walking. They all froze on the spot. Stuart and Holly turned to Corinna with panicked looks, unsure of what she'd seen. She was staring off to the left, just ahead of them, at one of the many thick bushes nestled between the trees. They followed her gaze. The bush was gently swaying as though something - or someone - had disturbed it. None of them said anything. They just stood there, in the open, waiting to see if anyone was going to come out for them.

"It was probably an animal," Stuart said. "A rabbit or something…" He was sure it wasn't a person but it didn't stop him from talking in a hushed voice. Just because he didn't think anyone was in the bush, it didn't mean they weren't close by.

"Do they have rabbits here?" Corinna asked.

Stuart shrugged. He didn't have a clue as to what animals were or weren't present in this area but - especially now of all times - he didn't really want to think about it. He just wanted to get out of there and back to the jeep. "Just keep moving," he said, taking the first step and leading the way. The girls walked with him, keeping side by side and close together. All of them looking like deer caught in the headlights.

The area closed in around them on all sides. The mud-track was soon entwined in vines and shrubs. It was on the other side of this little thicket that the man had attacked them and shot Jack with the arrow. Stuart pushed further ahead to try and clear a bit of a path for the girls. It had definitely been easier running through the thicket but they knew - whilst they were trying to be quiet - they had to try and move stealthily.

Stuart pulled back the last of the spindly branches, revealing the opening where they'd been attacked. He stopped causing the girls to bump into him. His eyes transfixed to something dead ahead. He turned his back on it and looked to the girls.

"What is it?" Holly whispered.

"Don't look!" he said. A hint of urgency in his voice which only made Holly (and Corinna) want to look more. Holly tried to peer around him but he pulled her close and hugged her tight. "Don't look, don't look, don't look…" he kept repeating the words again and again.

"What is it?" Holly asked. She was starting to panic as she struggled against his tight grip. In her head, she couldn't think of what could be so bad she wouldn't be allowed to see. A question which her own brain answered almost immediately. It was Jack. "Let me go!" She wasn't whispering anymore. Stuart released her knowing he had little choice. The more she was starting to panic, the louder she was becoming.

Corinna screamed. Stuart had been so busy trying to calm Holly, stop her from seeing what he'd seen, he hadn't realised Corinna had pushed past him. He spun around and covered her mouth with his hand to stifle her scream.

Holly's eyes went wide and instantly welled up. She didn't scream though as she took in what had alarmed both of her friends.

Jack.

Holly took a step forward and froze. Stuart released Corinna and blocked Holly's line of sight to Jack's body.

"The way out is down there," he said with a nod of his head towards where they'd originally come in. "We can just go. There's nothing we can do for him. I'm sorry."

"Get out of my way," she hissed. Despite Stuart standing in front of her, she was still staring ahead - as though looking through him. "I said get out of my fucking way!" she repeated herself when it was obvious he wasn't going to move.

He sighed, "There's nothing we can do," and stepped out of her way.

Holly didn't move. She was just standing there, shaking. Stuart didn't say anything. Nor did Corinna. There was nothing to say. Both of them wanted to leave. Get the hell out of there before anyone came back. Stuart was looking from side to side, checking all around on the off-chance Jack had been left there as a trap for them; paranoid that - at any minute - they were going to be ambushed. Holly took a step forward and gasped as she got a better look at her once-boyfriend. Stuart didn't look. He didn't want to despite wanting to know what she'd seen. Even Corinna wasn't looking at the body. Her eyes were shut tight. She too was shaking.

"We have to leave," Stuart pushed them both. The longer they stood there, the more danger they were in.

Holly didn't respond. She walked over to Jack's body with her hands raised to her mouth to stop herself from screaming out, tears cascading down her pale cheeks as she took in what they'd done to him. Gone were his eyes - both of them, just gaping holes where they'd once been. Blood was caked around his mouth - slightly opened - and she could see more blood pooling inside. His shirt was also saturated in blood. She lowered her hands as she slowly (somehow) came to terms with what had been done to him. All the cruel things she'd said in arguments playing - on repeat - in her mind as the tears continued to spill.

"Holly," Stuart tried to steal her attention again. "Holly, there's nothing we can do. If we stay here much longer…"

Jack coughed a fountain of blood from his mouth as he gasped a gargled breath. All three of his friends jumped.

#

The bottle of vodka lay on its side. There wasn't enough of the spirit left in it to cause it to spill over the neck and out of the bottle mouth, onto the concrete floor. Jack lay next to it, slumped over on his side with his red-eyes rolling to the back of his skull. He was conscious but only just. Holly and Stuart were either side of him, laughing. Obviously drunk, they were at least in a better shape than him.

"Help me get him up," Holly said. She was pulling Jack by his arm, trying to get him up off the floor but he was a dead weight. Stuart took a hold of his other arm and the pair managed to get him up off the floor at least. They just didn't manage to keep control of him as all three crashed to the floor again.

It was supposed to be a nice camping trip. It was meant to be a case of a few drinks, some marshmallows over a small fire after a tasty barbecue, but it hadn't gone to plan. Stuart's girlfriend - at the time - had gone to bed, annoyed that Stuart hadn't wanted to go with her because he wanted to keep drinking. The barbecue food burned because Jack took his eye off it to beg Holly into giving him a blow job back at their tent and… Well nothing really went to plan. And now this. Jack had drunk too much and was on the verge of losing consciousness by the campsite toilet block.

Holly and Stuart laughed as they rolled around on the floor trying to get themselves up. Holly was first to her feet, helping Stuart up soon after.

"Can we just get a blanket and leave him out here?" she asked, without a hint of guilt in her voice. No doubt helped by the copious amounts she herself had managed to drink that night.

Stuart shrugged, "Don't see why not. It's a clear night," he laughed. It was a clear night. Out in the middle of the country - at a popular camping site - you could see the stars filling the black sky and the brilliant white moon shining high, like a perfectly painted scene of bliss.

Holly laughed, "I'll get a blanket from the tent." She turned and hurried towards the small two-person tent they'd earlier assembled before the drinking had started. The front of the tent was open and she leaned in. Jack and Holly had laid out two sleeping bags. They were opened right up so as to form a makeshift duvet which they could snuggle under, as opposed to forcing them to sleep separately. One was to be used as a ground sheet and the second to be used as their main covering during the night. At the top were two pillows, taken from their beds at home, and - to the side of that - a blanket, rolled up, ready for if the night were to turn chilly. She grabbed the blanket and jumped when she turned back to the opening of the tent only to see Stuart standing there. He was smiling. A smile she recognised only too well.

"You made me jump," she laughed.

"Ssh." He edged into the tent and moved closer to her until they were face to face. "This is killing me," he said. She smiled as he put his arms around her waist and pulled her even closer. He leaned in and kissed her on the lips. She didn't resist. Another peck on the lips and the following kisses began to get more passionate, their tongues exploring each other's mouths. His hands moved to her arse, still keeping her close to him, and her own hands doing the same to him.

Holly pulled away, "We can't. Not here."

"Why not? He's comatose and…"

"She is sleeping in the next tent. What if she wakes up?"

"Who cares? I don't want her. I want you."

"I told you, I can't."

"Why not? You know you want it too…"

"I just… It's not fair on Jack."

"Like he's fair to you, you mean?" Stuart kissed her again. She didn't put up much of a fight and they were soon entwined in a passionate embrace once more. "You're so fucking hot. You're all I think about."

Holly shushed him quiet as she fumbled with the belt on his jeans, ready to free his bulge.

#

Holly couldn't take her eyes off Stuart as she tried to support Jack's weight. The position she found herself in now reminding her of that camping trip. She had one arm, he had the other. Corinna was flapping around them, panicking that the tribesmen would be coming back at any moment. Stuart had told her to keep a watch out for them, whilst they struggled to help Jack from the woodlands, back towards where they'd left the jeep.

The noise they were making was high now. Gone were the worries of being quiet. Now it was all about getting them out of the woods using any means necessary and - unfortunately - that meant a fair bit of noise as they struggled with their wounded friend. It didn't matter though. Even if they'd been quiet they'd have still been watched from the corner of the woods. Not just one pair of eyes but many. Not just one set of teeth but many. All hungry for the taste of flesh. All wondering whether this was the one who'd silence the Demons.

END OF PART ONE

INTERVAL

Splashing and screaming from the pool.

Parents calling out to their children in a mixture of different languages.

Sun beating down hard upon the black sands of the volcanic island.

Towels laid out for guests, some on loungers and some on the sand itself.

Waves lapping at the shoreline.

The sea is quiet.

Laughing echoing across the way.

A gentle breeze periodically shaking the leaves of the few palm trees planted for decorative purposes.

The sound of clinking glasses from across the way at the outside bar.

The sound of the barman, a friendly man with a broad smile, telling a group of young holidaymakers about this special beach.

There's white sands there.

Water that is - somehow - even clearer than at the resort.

No tourists there and not many locals either; most of the latter don't even know of its existence.

An offer of the use of the barman's vehicle; a battered old jeep.

Offer graciously accepted.

The excitement of venturing from the confines of the pleasant resort.

A need to spread their wings and explore locations unknown.

Glasses raised to the air and clinked together.

"Cheers!"

The barman smiles.

A distant clap of thunder from across the way, seemingly coming from behind the volcano.

The barman also raises a glass.

#

Corinna screamed. Holly turned and screamed too. The sight of all those men standing there, weapons raised, pointing towards them. They had just appeared out of nowhere. One minute everything was still and calm and the next, they were there. The hostile voices shouting at the foursome in a series of clicks and clacks. Stuart yelled at the girls; a panicked voice screaming to hurry as he continued dragging Jack towards the open space beyond the woods, forcing Holly to do the same.

The tribe didn't move from where they'd appeared on and around the various trees like a pack of animals stalking their prey. They just waited, shouting whatever it was they were yelling.

Stuart was first into the open, followed by Jack and Holly. Less than a second later, Corinna came running out - screaming, fearful of an arrow piercing her from behind just as it had done so with Jack.

"Where's the fucking jeep?" she screamed.

Stuart looked up expecting to see the vehicle where they'd left it. He'd presumed Corinna had simply glanced in the wrong direction, maybe turned around by the panic she was in. His heart skipped a beat when he realised she was right though. It had gone.

Their way out of this Hell was missing.

#

Barman hands the keys to one of the men in the group.

In return, notes are handed over.

The group sees the battered, dusty jeep and laugh at the expense of the one who paid.

History repeats itself.

Not for the first time.

PART TWO

6.

Stuart let go of Jack's arm, as did Holly. Jack slumped to the floor. They weren't sure if he was unconscious again, or dead. He'd been quiet since dragging him from the forest. It didn't matter now. If he wasn't already dead, he soon would be. They all would. They turned back to the woodlands where Corinna was already looking; tears streaming down her petrified face and her legs trembling violently.

The tribesmen had gathered at the entrance to the forest. Black eyes all staring at the friends with a look of hatred and intent burning from within their tainted souls.

"Leave us alone!" Corinna screamed at them as loudly as she could. In part to try and scare them off and in part to alert anyone nearby that they were in danger. No one would be coming, even if they had been there. They'd have simply turned around and carried on with their business. This was nothing new to them; just another day in paradise.

Stuart took a step closer to the natives. A genuine look of concern written all over his face. He raised his hands to show he had no concealed weapons and wasn't a threat to them, even though it was them who were the threat. He was well aware he was nothing but 'the easy target'.

"What are you doing?" Corinna asked.

"We don't mean any harm," he called out to the tribe. They stopped their chatter and listened. He wasn't sure whether they were just mesmerised by the sound of his language or whether they could understand him but he continued regardless. After all, the way he saw it, he didn't really have much of a choice. "If we trespassed on your land, we are very sorry. That wasn't our intention. We meant no offense." He paused. One of the tribesmen called out; those damned clicks and clacks and little else that made any kind of sense. "I'm sorry!" Stuart said when the man fell silent, "I don't understand you! Please, just let us go home. We're sorry but this doesn't have to go any further…" The tribe started to laugh. Stuart took a step back as the realisation hit, these were not nice people.

"What should we do?" Holly asked him. There was a desperation in her voice hoping he might have the answer for her. He didn't. He had no idea what they should do. The only thing going around and around in his head was the wish they'd gone on another skiing vacation. He turned to her with a vacant look on his face. What could they do? There was no vehicle there. They were miles from anywhere. There was nowhere for them to run, not that they could outrun arrows.

Stuart turned back to the people watching from the trees. They were still quietly chattering amongst themselves. "Let them go and take me," he said.

"No!" Corinna shouted although - if push came to shove - it would have most likely been an okay scenario for her.

The tribesmen didn't acknowledge what was offered. Stuart made the same offer again in the hope they'd understand him if he said it for a second time. Again, they showed no signs of having done so.

He screamed, "What do you fucking want with us?" The frustration and fear taking their toll. He had apologised for going into their territory, he said it wouldn't happen again. He offered himself in exchange for the girls, no fighting on his part and still nothing - they were just standing there, watching them with smiles on their faces. Without a word one of the tribesmen stepped forward from the rest of the group. "Yes," Stuart encouraged him. "Please. Tell me what you want."

The stranger raised his hand and pointed his finger to Holly. She responded by backing up and bursting into tears.

"What?" Stuart followed the man's finger and then turned back to him. "You can't have her. I said take me and let them go. You can't have them."

Corinna started to back away. In her selfish mind, she was in the clear. They didn't want her. She could go. One of the other tribesmen shouted something at her which instantly made her root to the spot. A harshness in his voice emphasised with the raising of a wooden spear, sharpened to a point.

"Don't fucking move!" Stuart hissed at Corinna. "Just stay there! Don't fucking make it worse than it already is!"

"What's worse?" she argued. "They killed him! They're going to kill us!"

Stuart ignored her. He turned back to the one he presumed was leading them, "Please take me and let them go. I won't fight you. I'll do whatever you want."

The man pointed again at Holly.

"I don't want to die," she wept.

"That's not going to happen!" Stuart said.

The tribesman pointed again and shouted something. He beckoned Holly over to the trees.

"I said she's not fucking going with you!" Stuart yelled.

From the tree-line an arrow was aimed at him. He immediately put his hands up higher in the air to show he wasn't a threat to them. The supposed leader yelled again towards Holly, waving her over once more.

"If I come, you'll let them go. Okay?" Holly said.

"What are you doing?" Stuart asked. He didn't take his eyes from the man pointing the arrow at him. A tall native who looked to be in his forties, maybe a little older. Both of his black eyes piercing Stuart's soul. "Don't you move, Holly. Don't you fucking move! We can fix this…"

"There's nothing to fix," she said.

From where they were all standing it was obvious the natives were going to get what they wanted but it didn't mean Stuart wasn't holding out some hope for a miracle. Maybe someone would come by and rescue them? Maybe? In his head he heard his inner devil laughing at the thought of being rescued. No one was coming. No one was going to rescue them. They were already dead and they were just delaying the inevitable.

Holly took a step closer towards the trees. Stuart blocked her path, an action which angered the waiting tribesmen. He ignored their shouting as he begged her not to go to them, reminding her what they'd done to Jack.

"I have to," she said. "At least this way you can go. Get help and bring them here…"

"They haven't made any promises they're letting any of us go!" he pointed out.

"If she wants to go, just let her!" Corinna said. Stuart looked at her in disgust. This was the woman he thought he loved, after Holly anyway. He thought she was a good person, a caring one, and yet this whole situation - although extreme - proved she was only out for herself. "I don't want to die here," Corinna said when she noticed Stuart's look.

"We stick together. I'm not leaving you with these savages!" Stuart turned back to Holly.

"They want me. They don't want you. They might let you go."

"And they might not."

"What else are we going to do?" Holly said. It was clear from her expression that she was open to suggestions. But it was also clear from the expressions of both Stuart and Corinna that they had no further suggestions as to how best to handle the situation. "I don't have a choice. This is the only thing I can do, go peacefully with them in the hope they let you go."

"I don't want…"

"Please don't make this harder than it already is," Holly interrupted Stuart.

More shouting from behind Stuart reminded him that people were waiting. Not just waiting but getting impatient. Holly took another step forward and - once again - Stuart went to block her path.

"I won't let you do this," he said. "I can't…" before another word escaped his mouth he screamed out loud and fell to the floor, backwards. Both Holly and Corinna screamed. Immediately they saw the arrow sticking from the back of his leg. Shouting from the tree-line pulled their attention towards the hostile natives. The one standing out from the rest of the group had his bow raised and a large smile on his face. He'd been the one who'd fired the arrow.

Corinna dropped down to her knees, next to Stuart. She put her hand around the arrow and went to pull it out, "I'll help you!" she said.

"Don't! Leave it in there!" Stuart shouted, panicked she'd ignore him and pull it out anyway - thus increasing the flow of lost blood. "Shit it hurts!"

Corinna released the arrow, not knowing what to do for the best. The man who had fired the arrow shouted again. Neither Corinna nor Stuart needed to look up to know he was shouting for Holly's attention.

"I'm sorry," Holly said to her friends. "I don't have a choice!"

Stuart screamed out for her to stop as she started walking towards the tribe. The man - standing out from the group - put his bow over his shoulder and extended his hand towards her. He called out again as Holly continued to walk towards him. When she was close enough, the man grabbed her roughly by the arm and dragged her back towards the trees.

Stuart screamed out again, "No! Holly! Don't! I love you!" His words echoed through the open space. His words echoed through Corinna's soul. She turned to him, a look of both shock and disgust on her face as his words sunk in. Stuart didn't notice. If he did, he didn't pay any attention. His eyes were fixed on the bushes Holly had been dragged into. Suddenly he noticed four natives heading towards him as he lay upon the dirty ground. As they neared, he sat up in the hope it would be a better position with which to defend himself.

Corinna turned and ran from them. Two chased whilst the other two continued towards Stuart. One raised his long spear.

"Fuck..." was all Stuart managed to say before the spear was smacked across his face, knocking him clean out cold. Corinna screamed as one of the natives caught up with her and grabbed her from behind. There was never a deal to take one and let the others go. They wanted one of the group but it didn't mean they couldn't use all of them...

#

There was a hint of concern buried deep within Holly's early morning tone. Hidden well somewhere beneath her stifled laughter as she - once again - tried to wake Jack up from his previous night's drunken stupor. Holly hadn't realised Stuart had crept out of the tent, she'd slipped into a comfortable state of unconsciousness more or less as soon as they'd finished. When she woke, and he was nowhere to be seen, she'd simply presumed he had crept back through to his own tent where his girlfriend had disappeared earlier that night. She hadn't realised he'd paid Jack a little visit first.

They'd given him a blanket before succumbing to their lust for one another. They had simply thrown it over him and made sure he was lying on his side, on the off-chance he was sick during the night - as he was prone to do after a heavy session. Seeing him this morning, though, it was clear he had been…. tampered with…. during the night. The blanket was still over his body but - on top of that - were all of the cans they'd managed to polish off as a group during the evening. And it wasn't just limited to cans. All of the rubbish from the disastrous barbecue was thrown in a pile on top of him too and his face, and hands, had been 'decorated' with…

"What is that?" Holly turned to Stuart who was sitting by the dying campfire. He looked bad this morning. The heavy abuse of alcohol the previous night had clearly taken its toll of him as he appeared to nurse one of the worst hangovers he'd ever suffered.

"Where's my lipstick?" Stuart's girlfriend called from within her tent.

Holly and Stuart couldn't help but laugh.

"You know she's going to kill you, right?" Holly laughed at Stuart. He shrugged. He'd broken his partner's lipstick by wearing it down completely; writing a barrage of filth over any visible part of Jack's body. 'Prick' and 'asshole' being two of the tamer words. Holly bit her bottom lip as she stifled another laugh when she looked back to the man she was supposed to love. "He might kill you too."

"Especially if he knew what happened last night," Stuart said. Holly turned to him, in a panic, and put her finger up to her mouth to quieten Stuart down.

The last thing she needed was for Jack to hear a part of the conversation. Last night shouldn't have happened (again). She didn't regret it. She loved Stuart. At least she thought she did. For all she knew it could have been a case of the grass being greener on the other side. It didn't mean she wanted Jack to find out like that though. She wanted to be the one to tell him when she was good and ready. She turned back to her sleeping man. Seeing him like this, and in the state he'd managed to get himself into the previous night, she often wondered what she originally had originally had seen in him. Sure Stuart wasn't the perfect man but he was ten times better than this. At least Stuart only got into this state on rare occasions. With Jack it was every weekend, more or less. Not that he ever seemed to have a reason as to why it was so entirely necessary to get blind-drunk!

The tent Stuart was supposed to have slept in opened up and his girlfriend poked her head out from between the flaps, "Stuart, did you hear me? Have you seen my lipstick?"

"Sorry, love. Not seen it," he lied, flashing Holly a little wink.

Holly turned her attention back to Jack. He was still out like a light despite the fact they weren't exactly whispering around him and other nearby camping spots were a hive of activity; children screaming and hot breakfasts cooking on the camp stoves, filling the air with the gorgeous scent of bacon and eggs.

"Wake up!" Holly gave Jack a shake. He groaned but still didn't open his eyes. She shook him again and kept calling his name until - eventually - he opened his bloodshot eyes. From the moment he first looked at her, a confused look upon his face, it was clear he'd be suffering from one of the worst hangovers. Holly sighed. She didn't mind him drinking but when it had an impact on the day after, meaning they couldn't do anything together, it pissed her off. Not that it made any difference. "Wake up!" she shouted in his face hoping the sudden fright would get his brain firing on all cylinders.

#

"Wake up!" Holly screamed. "Wake up!" Holly called out again. A frantic cry aimed towards Stuart as he lay unconscious on the floor next to the wooden stake he was soon to be strapped to, just as she and Corinna had been. If only he could wake up now, he might have a chance to make a run for it. Maybe he'd be able to get some help? There were only a couple of the natives restraining the friends. Their weapons leaning on the side of a hut on the opposite side of the clearing. He'd have enough time to make a run for the trees. He just needed to wake up. Holly called out to him again but was slapped silent by one of the men. His harsh back-hander across the face was accompanied with - what she presumed to be - equally harsh words; a warning to keep quiet no doubt. Holly did fall silent but it didn't stop her from willing him to wake up. Please, God, just wake up.

The second of the men finished securing Corinna to the wooden stake next to the one Holly had been tied to. A large pole - sticking from the ground - at least six feet high. God only knew how deep it was dug in but both girls knew, from the moment their backs were pushed against it, it was down enough not to be toppled. He said something to his friend (were they friends Holly wondered) and the two of them grabbed the still unconscious Stuart before dragging him to the third pole. They pulled him up so that his back was also against it and - as one held him there to stop him sliding onto his side - the other started binding him with what appeared to be some kind of strong vine, fashioned into a rope by wrapping several pieces around each other.

As the vines were fastened, trapping him into place, the two girls began to weep once more. Their chance of one of them - at least - getting away had slipped from their grasp. Not that it was ever really within reach in the first place.

The girls didn't say anything as the two natives took a step back and admired their handiwork. They were both smiling. Not the kind of smile which filled you with much joy, or hope, but rather the kind that filled you with dread. The man standing on Holly's right (and closest to Corinna) pointed at Corinna and said something to the man standing with him. They both laughed, turned, and walked back towards the hut.

"What did they say?" Corinna asked. She was panicking. And why wouldn't she? She'd been pointed out by one of the men who'd taken her prisoner. She didn't know why. All she knew was it couldn't be a good thing, to have the attention of one of the people keeping you against your will. "What did they say?" she asked Holly again, as though she'd learned the language in the last couple of hours.

"I don't know," Holly said. "I don't know." Instead of sitting there, worrying about it, she started to fight against the vines binding her to the stake. Having seen the state of Jack, she knew she couldn't afford to just sit there and wait for them to come back. "Stuart, wake up!" she hissed. With the stakes being close enough together, she tried to kick across to him in an effort to stir him from the sleep. Just how hard did they hit him?

7.

Corinna screamed out loud and kicked out only to be stopped by the people attempting to hold her down. They'd pulled her from the stake they'd bound her to and dragged her towards a fire two of the female natives had set up. She screamed for Holly to help her as they each took it in turns to rip off her clothes but Holly could do nothing but weep for her friend as she watched the horrors take place before her eyes. A little part of her thankful they'd chosen Corinna instead of her. A little part dreading what they had in mind when her turn came. Corinna screamed out again, a cry of fear which finally pulled Stuart from his enforced slumber. Immediately he started to struggle against the vines holding him against the stake.

"What the fuck is going on?" he asked as panic set in. It took no time for the memories of what was happening to them to come flooding back to him. "Get the fuck off of her, you cunts!" Stuart started shouting at the tribesmen in the hope they'd stop. He knew they wouldn't. "Leave her alone!" Even kicking up some of the dry dirt from the ground didn't deter them, not that he thought for one minute that it would.

"Please! Don't!" Corinna's own screams cut through Stuart's soul. The pain in her voice. The desperation. The fear. "Let me go! Please!" Now completely naked, she turned her head to Stuart and Holly and screamed again, "I don't want to die!"

Stuart wanted to tell her that she wouldn't. He wanted to say that everything was going to be okay but he knew he couldn't. It would have been a lie. There was nothing either he or Holly could do for her.

A larger tribesman came out of the hut. He had with him a large pole, similar to the ones keeping Holly and Stuart on the floor. Both ends had been sharpened. He glanced to both Holly and Stuart with a look of pure burning hatred in his eyes. Without a word, he turned his attention back to the naked girl held down by other members of his tribe and slowly walked over to them.

"Fuck you!" Corinna shouted at him as she saw him heading over. "Fuck you!"

Stuart realised what was happening and told Holly, "Close your eyes."

"What are they doing?" she asked. She repeated the sentence again, more panicked this time, "What are they doing?"

"Please. Just close your eyes," Stuart said. Despite his instruction to Holly, he didn't follow his own advice. He kept watching as four of the tribe pinned the petrified girl down on the ground. "Close your eyes!" he said once more.

Holly closed them tight.

Sometimes when you close your eyes you can take yourself away from horrible situations. You can take yourself somewhere better. But not when the sounds were still perfectly audible. Holly wished her hands were free so that she could cover her ears. She wished she could drown out the high pitched screaming. A soul-destroying, hope crushing sound which painted a picture just as horrible as if Holly had witnessed what was causing it. And what was it that was causing the screaming?

Stuart couldn't take his eyes off what was happening despite telling Holly to keep hers closed. Corinna was trying to thrash about in obvious discomfort. She was stopped only by the powerful grip of the men pinning her in place as the other man pushed the spiked shaft deep into her vagina. The further in it was pushed, the higher pitched the screaming.

Stuart was shouting out for them to stop. He was begging them to let her go and stop doing what they were doing but his words were ignored. He wondered if they even heard him over the sound of Corinna's screaming. He wished - if they had to carry on - that they'd speed the process up but they were making no signs of doing so. Slowly pushing the pole bit by bit as though there was some resistance inside.

"What's happening?" Holly cried out, still with her eyes screwed shut.

"Don't you fucking look. Keep your eyes closed!" Stuart said. Instructions which sounded more as though he were begging her to do as he said. He tried to make it sound more authoritative to give her more reason to listen, "Don't you fucking open your eyes!"

Corinna's scream changed pitch once more. She nodded her head forward with a jolt of pain as the pole pierced her cervix and continued up into her stomach. The man controlling it pulled it out a fraction before pushing forward again, ripping up her insides until it was tearing into her lungs - turning them to mush in the process. She coughed up some blood and her head fell back to the bloody ground. Her limbs were still attempting to thrash around despite being held firmly but the screaming had stopped now as the last of her soul escaped her tortured body. Stuart gagged when he realised he'd just witnessed the death of his girlfriend. He turned away a moment, with his eyes shut, hoping not to follow through by vomiting over himself.

Go to a happy place.

Go to a happy place.

Go to a happy place.

#

Four youths, two men and two girls, were laughing as they tore across the deserted streets in the borrowed jeep. A thick plume of blue, stinking smoke billowing from the tailpipe. A gas station rolled into sight across the horizon as one of the girls pointed it to the male driver. The jeep slowed before it turned into the poor excuse of a forecourt. It stopped at the first pump it came to - not that there were many to choose from. The passengers emptied from the claustrophobic vehicle, not that they'd been in it long enough for their bones to start cramping. A man came running out of the small shack-like shop and proceeded to pump the gas for them. He was all smiles as he spoke with three of the visitors. His dark eyes fixed upon one of the girls. Only one of the foursome wasn't listening to a word he said.

Only one of them had spotted something and was staring across the road: a donkey, hacked into pieces, had bled out opposite from where they were standing.

#

Go to a happy place.

Go to a happy place… There were no happy places.

Not anymore.

This was all there was.

The two men at the top end of Corinna's limp body lifted her from the floor slightly so that she was now at an angle. The man with the control of the pole thrust forward and there was a god awful crack before the pole tore from Corinna's neck and out of her open mouth. The man grunted again and pushed forward one final time so that an equal amount of the pole was protruding from both ends of Corinna. The men all switched positions so that two of them were at the top end of the pole (coming from the mouth) and two were at the bottom end (coming from the vagina). They seemingly counted down in their language before - together - they hoisted her up from the ground. With minimal effort they moved her over the fire and secured her in place by resting either end of the pole into ready-made slots. Her long hair, her arms, and her legs hung down into the wild licking flames until her limbs were fastened to her body with strong vines. Only the hair remained burning.

"What's that smell?" Holly asked, still too afraid to open her eyes.

Stuart didn't say anything. There was nothing he could say. She had her eyes closed now but he knew it was only a matter of time before she opened them. It was inevitable. There was no hiding what was happening.

As the stink of toasting flesh and burning hair filled the air - and their nostrils - he whispered to Holly, "I love you." It wasn't the most romantic of settings and he didn't expect her to say it back. But it still needed saying. For all he knew, it would be his last chance. He smiled - for what felt like the first time in a while - when she whispered it back.

The four tribesmen left Corinna hanging over the fire as they walked past the hut and through to what must have been the rest of the camp. Stuart seized the opportunity to warn Holly for what she'd see when she opened her eyes.

"Don't open your eyes yet," he told her softly, "but you need to know what's happened. They've gone. They've killed Corinna and..." he took a deep breath as there was no easy way of saying it, "That smell... She's over the fire. They're fucking cooking her..."

"What?" Holly began to cry again as shock set in once more. She opened her eyes and wept louder when she saw Corinna hanging over the fire. Her skin already red from the intensity of the heat. "Why are they doing this?" she asked, desperately trying not to scream.

"I don't know," he said, "but, like I've said, they've gone now. We can't just sit here waiting for them to come back. We have to try and get away…" as he spoke, he was trying to loosen the vines holding him to the stake by wriggling his body from side to side. "See if you can shake them loose too," he urged Holly to do the same. He knew the likelihood of getting out of the bindings was low. The way the natives were working together, it was obvious they had done this kind of thing on numerous occasions. With that in mind, the chances of them failing to tie one of their prisoners properly was slim to none. But it didn't stop them from trying.

Stuart looked up in an effort to see the top of the pole. Had it been short enough he figured he might have been able to stand up and maybe jump high enough to disconnect himself. Looking now, though, he realised that was never going to happen. Clearly something else they had thought about.

"It won't move," Holly said, pointing out the obvious.

"Just keep trying!" Stuart huffed as he did as he'd instructed her. If he was going to die, he was going to do so fighting. He refused to just sit there and wait to be cooked, or whatever else they had in mind.

A hostile voice calling from beyond the fire, somewhere in the trees, made both Stuart and Holly jump. A second voice stopped them from fighting against the restraints. Across the way, close to the fire, one of the many bushes parted and two men stepped into the clearing. One looked the same as all the others had done but the other, his face was decorated in paint of mixed colours and hanging from his neck was a string with small bone fragments.

"Don't move," Stuart whispered to Holly, not that he had to. She'd already frozen at the first sound of their voices. Her heart beating so fast that Stuart could hear it. "Stay calm. Whatever happens, stay calm." It was easier said than done. They'd both seen what had happened to their friends. Neither activity looked to be particularly pleasant. Under those kinds of circumstances, no one would have been able to stay calm.

"I'm scared," Holly said quietly. Stuart tried to be brave. He tried to give her a reassuring glance. He tried to hide the fact he was scared too. "Promise me you won't leave me," she said.

"I promise."

It hadn't been the first time he'd made such a promise. But it was the first time he hadn't been sure as to whether he could keep it or not.

#

"I'm scared," said Holly. She was standing in Jack's living room, in the small apartment he shared with Stuart. Jack wasn't there. Stuart was sitting on the settee, leaning forward. His eyes were fixed intently upon Holly.

"You can't be."

"Well I am."

"It'll be fine, we'll do it together."

"He's going to be so angry," Holly said. She was referring to Jack and how he'd react upon hearing the news she'd slept with his best friend after one too many drinks. "What if he doesn't forgive me?" she asked.

Stuart frowned and shifted in his seat awkwardly, "Would you want him to?" he asked.

"I love him."

Her words hit Stuart hard and he swallowed his emotions down. It was clear she thought it was a one night stand, what had happened between them, but in his head it had been so much more. It had been what he wanted right from the moment he'd first met her. That day when Jack brought her home and introduced the two. She was standing there, smiling so sweetly. He had been instantly smitten.

"What if I said I loved you?" he asked.

"What?"

"From the very first moment I met you," he continued without getting up. He didn't want her to feel backed into a corner, he didn't want her to feel uncomfortable but he had to get his thoughts off his chest. "Your smile, your eyes... Everything is just perfect to me and you have no idea how much it bugs me seeing him treat you the way he does."

Holly didn't say anything to him. She just sat there, dumbstruck. After the skiing accident... After what had happened between them... She thought it had been a one off. She thought it was only because they were drunk. She never realised he had these feelings for her. She didn't know what to say to him.

"Nothing to say?" he pushed her. "Don't have any thoughts about any of that?" he asked.

She hesitated a moment before saying, "I'm with Jack."

Stuart's heart sunk. From the moment they'd woken up, the following morning, she had been the only thing on his mind. There had been nothing else. During this time, he'd managed to convince himself that they'd become a couple. They'd be together. He hadn't expected the brush off. "Right," he said, "of course... I'm sorry," he tried to save face.

"Please you can't tell him what happened."

"I won't."

"It was a mistake."

Another knife to Stuart's heart.

"I won't say anything."

"Promise?"

"I promise." He wanted to be with her but not enough to break up the relationship. He could have easily told Jack what had happened but it wouldn't have done anything but anger him and upset Holly and he didn't want that. He wanted her to leave Jack for her own reasons, not because he discovered what happened and booted her out of the relationship. He swallowed the hurt down and concentrated on setting his mind to someone else, someone not in a relationship, completely unaware that, despite what she said, their drunken fling was the first of many.

"Thank you," she said.

He smiled at her despite feeling crushed.

#

As the smell of burning flesh continued to pollute the atmosphere, the two natives continued to cross the clearing towards their captive prisoners. Their eyes were fixed upon Holly. As they neared, one pulled a machete from where it hung in a small hand-made holder. He raised it into the air and slammed it into the side of Holly's stake, cutting the vines that bound her there. The other man barked something at her. She didn't move. Rooted to the spot with fear and confused as to what they wanted to her. The second man made it more obvious by pulling her to her feet.

"Where are you taking her?" Stuart yelled.

The two natives ignored him as they dragged Holly towards the bushes from where they'd just come. Stuart continued to yell at them as Holly called back to him, begging for him to help her.

He was powerless.

8.

Stuart was alone. He wasn't sure how much time had passed now. The sun was starting to go down. The roar of the fire seemed to be going down. Corinna was practically black and had been pulled away from the fire and dumped on the floor unceremoniously. Natives came and went, all of whom ignored Stuart. Instead they were more interested in Corinna and were using machete blades to peel away some of her burnt skin before putting it their mouths and chewing enthusiastically. A look of appreciation on their faces which disgusted Stuart more than the act of what they were actually doing.

He called out to them, "What have you done with my friend?"

They didn't even look at him. They just carried on helping themselves to 'dinner' and walking back through to the other area, out of sight. First the men and then, when they stopped coming, the women.

The women paid more attention to Stuart. With handfuls of Corinna, they approached him as though curious about him. There was no fear in their eyes. There was no sign of them being uncomfortable at his presence or how he looked.

"What have you done with my friend?" he asked again on the off-chance one of them could understand or even tell him where Holly had been taken. They said nothing though.

One of the girls - a topless woman who looked to be in her twenties - crouched down next to Stuart. She took a handful of Corinna from her hand and handed it towards Stuart's mouth.

"Fuck off," he hissed.

Realising he didn't want it, the woman pulled it away and threw it into her mouth. Stuart watched as the meat circled around in her mouth gradually getting more and more mushed up in the process. He turned his head to the side and gagged as the woman dribbled a bit out onto Stuart's legs. She laughed and scooped it back up, slurping it up from the palm of her hand. Stuart gagged again and vomited to the side of where he was trapped; an action which only seemed to excite the women around him. One girl wasted no time in dunking her pieces of dinner into the small puddle of sick before licking it up into her mouth with a sound of approval.

Slurp.

Stuart gagged again and resisted the urge to vomit once more. He closed his eyes and once again tried to take himself away from the situation but just as Holly had struggled earlier, when listening to Corinna scream, he too failed. The sounds of the chewing and lips smacking together, the knowledge what it was in their mouths... It all become too much and he screamed out loud.

"What have you done with my friend?"

His answer was hidden with the sound of giggling. A male voice barked from a distance away and the girls instantly stopped giggling as they scattered in all directions. Stuart opened his eyes and saw the tall, skinny man standing close to the fire. Just as everyone else had, he too had helped himself to a handful of meat - resembling pulled pork - from the charred body of Corinna. The skinny freak was standing there, staring at Stuart with a look of hatred in his eyes.

In what appeared to be a couple of steps only, the native covered the distance from the burnt body to where Stuart was tied. He leaned down so that he was face to face with him. He didn't say anything. He just stared at him, eye to eye. Stuart seized the opportunity to try again with the language barrier.

"Please, just let me go."

The native smiled and said something. That damned series of clicks and pops. He threw the palmful of meat over his shoulder and winked to Stuart. What was he saying? As soon as he finished he leaned forward and licked Stuart's face. Stuart flinched but couldn't get away. He closed his eyes and tried - once again - to think of a happy place. The native pulled away and licked his lips. Another series of clicks, clacks, and pops of his tongue as he said something. Stuart turned to him and spat in the man's face. The native laughed and wiped the dribble from his cheek before standing to his full height.

"Make it quick!" Stuart told him, expecting an unpleasant death to be following.

The tribesman reached behind him and withdrew a long machete from its hand-made scabbard. Stuart closed his eyes. If this was to be it, he didn't want to see it coming. Another undeciphered conversation and then Stuart heard the sound of steel slicing air; a whooshing noise... And then he felt everything around him go loose. The vines. He opened his eyes and the native was putting the machete back in its holder; a smile on his face. He clenched his fist and shouted something at Stuart.

Was he really challenging him?

Stuart shook the rest of the vines off and stood up, almost buckling right back down again due to the wound in his leg. His mind was swayed in two directions. The first being to run. Just fucking run. Head for the trees and don't look back. But would he get far with his leg? The second was to stand his ground and fight but what if he did? Was the skinny man as weak as he looked? What if he called out and the others come running?

The native beckoned Stuart to come towards him. Stuart just stood there a moment, still mentally weighing up the options. The man clenched his fists together in preparation for a fight. Stuart took up the fighting stance and did the same. His left arm held out slightly in front of his right as though he were some kind of professional boxer. The native lowered his defenses and frowned at Stuart. More clicks of the tongue. Stuart looked puzzled as he started to laugh. And then, in the blink of an eye, the skinny man's face turned from laughter to anger as he withdrew his machete and sliced upwards hard and fast. Stuart screamed as his left arm dropped to the ground, fist still clenched, and a fountain of blood erupted from the fresh wound. He fell to his knees and onto his back as the blood continued to spray the surrounding mud.

A low rumble of thunder shook the skies as the blood soaked into the earth. The native looked to the sky and shouted something before turning his attention back to Stuart. Stuart had rolled onto his front and was trying to drag himself away with his good arm. The native shook his head, grabbed Stuart's ankles, and pulled him back towards where he was standing - pulling his shorts down in the process, exposing his bare arse.

The native knelt down, pinning Stuart, and pulled his black cock from underneath his loin cloth. He stayed there, as Stuart continued to struggle (and bleed) beneath him, stroking it into an erection. Despite the blood he was losing, Stuart continued to scream out although his voice was definitely getting weaker. The native spat in his hand and rubbed his saliva over the tip of his cock before nudging it against Stuart's asshole. By now there wasn't much fight in Stuart. He was conscious but barely so and the blood spewing from the wound of his arm was definitely slowing in pace too. He grunted as the native thrust inside of him. The skinny man adjusted his position for a better depth of penetration and then started fucking Stuart hard.

Stuart closed his eyes.

Go to the better place.

The native groaned and sighed with each deep, ripping thrust.

Go to the better place.

Clicks of the tongue and pops of the mouth as the native whispered 'sweet nothings' to Stuart as he continued to fade.

Go to the better place.

Sighs, murmurs, grunts of satisfaction.

Go to the better place.

A cock so deep it felt as though it was pushing into Stuart's stomach.

Go to the better place.

The sting as each push ripped a little more internally.

Go to the better place.

The blood was but a trickle now.

Go to the better place.

A quickened, more painful pace as the native worked towards his orgasm.

Go to the better place.

A loud groan as the man shuddered and a stream of hot semen fired into Stuart's broken arse.

Go to the better place.

The man withdrew his cock, leaving a trail of spunk hanging from the end of it. He wiped the shit from the tip of it with the pink palm of his hand before licking that clean and laughing. Out of breath he stood up, letting his shrinking penis slip back underneath the protection of his loin cloth. He looked down at Stuart. He wasn't moving.

#

"You can't tell him," Holly said, "he'll kill you."

"You said it yourself, you want to be with me. You don't want to be with him anymore. I want to be with you. I'm fed up going from girl to girl trying to find someone who compares to you. I want you… So I have to tell him. We have to tell him."

"Let me tell him."

"He's my friend. It will sound better coming from me."

"No it won't. Being dumped by your girlfriend's lover is not better than being dumped by your actual girlfriend. I know he can be an idiot from time to time but I owe that much to him. Just maybe not tonight…"

"Then when?"

Stuart and Holly were sitting in Stuart's car. They were parked in the driveway. Stuart had offered to pop to the pizza shop to grab them all some dinner and Holly offered to go with him whilst Jack finished watching the end of the football game. As it usually did when it was the two of them together, the conversation hadn't taken long to turn to what they were doing with their on-off relationship. What had been a drunken fling had turned into an 'any opportunity' kind of affair. They both knew they wanted to be together. It was just telling Jack. Make the break and then they could be together. In conversations, it was always easy. But whenever the opportunity arose to follow through with their plans, they never seemed to come to fruition. Something which annoyed the hell out of Stuart who was growing ever more impatient.

"I just need to find the right time."

"There will never be a right time to do it. We just need to tell him. If you want, we can do it together," Stuart continued to push her.

"I don't want to ruin what we have…"

"What we have? The odd sneaky session here and there, you mean?" Stuart said. He wasn't knocking the times they had together but it was definitely clear he wanted more. "Let's just go in and tell him now. Get it over and done with."

"No!" Holly put her foot down. "I'm not ready yet. And I need to tell him by myself. You know he'll only kick off if you're there and I don't want you beating each other senseless over me," she sunk back in the passenger seat. "This whole thing is a mess."

Stuart tried to pacify her, "Okay we don't have to tell him yet. But I don't want to wait forever. I want to be with you. I can't make it any more obvious. I don't want to sneak around and just steal what I can when he isn't looking. And I'll make this promise to you…"

"What's that?"

"When the time comes, if you tell him when I am present and he does kick off… I promise I won't retaliate. I'll just play dead until he goes away. How's that?"

Holly smiled. If only it were that simple, she thought.

If only it were that simple…

"Anyway," Holly said turning the conversation away from Jack, "what about you and your new lady?"

"Corinna?"

"You'd need to tell her too."

"It's been a few weeks, maybe a month… It's considered a new relationship to most people. I mean it's not like you and Jack have spent more time with her. It won't take much to break things off with her. I just…" he hesitated.

"What?"

"Don't get mad…"

"What is it?" Holly pushed him.

"Promise me you won't get mad."

"I can't until you tell me what you were about to say! It might be something really offensive."

"Okay well… I don't want to break things off with her just for you to not tell Jack again. I like Corinna. She's a nice girl. But I want you and until you're ready for us to be an official couple… Well she's better than nothing." As soon as he finished explaining he turned to Holly to gauge her reaction. He half expected her to be upset. A part of him hoped a little jealous even. But she nodded as though she understood exactly where he was coming from. He continued, "Like I said, as soon as you're ready for us to become a proper item - not hiding anymore - I'll tell her and she will be out of the picture but, you know, we need to tell Jack first. We've been playing this dance for a few months now."

"I know."

"And I mean it. If we tell him and he gets aggressive… I'll play dead."

#

Stuart wasn't moaning. He wasn't in discomfort. The native kicked him with his left foot

- a gentle tap. Clicks of the tongue. Another kick. Stuart didn't open his eyes. For now he was unconscious but soon - most likely in less than a couple of minute's time - he'd be gone.

He'd have gone to the better place. And it wouldn't be long until Holly joined him.

Holly screamed as she broke away from the grip of the man escorting her up the mountain pass. They'd stopped long enough for the tribesman with the face-paint to point out a small river of lava in a crack in the mountain. He'd pointed to it and said something in his native tongue. Holly had had no idea what he was saying and didn't care. Up to that point, both men had been holding an arm each but then it was just one man holding onto her and she had been able to tell - from the way his hand was placed on her bare skin - that he didn't have the best of grips. She pulled up, spun on the spot and started running back in the direction she'd been led - holding her hands up to her face to protect against the bushes, twigs, and branches they'd previously navigated.

No sooner had she taken flight did she hear the angry yells of the two men who'd been leading her up the mountain. She didn't look back though. She didn't want to know what they were doing. She didn't want to know how close they were to catching up with her. She just wanted to run.

As she continued snaking her way through the undergrowth, down the pass - back in the direction she'd originally come - she kept expecting to feel the sudden jolt of pain pierce her skin from one of the many arrows she'd seen some of the men carry with them but there was nothing. She couldn't even hear the sound of footsteps behind her, nor the sound of chattering as they called instructions out between themselves on how best to capture her. There was the sound of her own footsteps stamping on the mud beneath her feet, snapping the various twigs, and crunching the many rocks as the pass had become more 'rocky' the further they had headed up the mountain trail. Other than that - the only sounds were her heavy, out of breath, breathing and the thump thump of her panicked heart-beat as the adrenaline continued surging through her body.

Don't look back, she kept telling herself. Don't look back.

EPILOGUE

The jeep turned down the narrow track and started towards the supposed beach of Paradise, unaware they were to encounter duller, black sand and less of the pure white grains they'd been promised by the barman of their resort.

One of the girls leaned forward and pointed to a large empty clearing in front of the lines of trees at the base of the volcano, "Look!" she said.

The driver, Alex, slammed on the brakes in panic that she'd seen something he hadn't.

"See it?"

"What?" the second girl asked, looking out of the back window.

"That clearing. According to island legend, that's where they used to sacrifice people to appease the demons in the belly of the volcano," the girl went on to explain. "By giving them sacrifices, the demons were stopped from destroying the island with an eruption."

Alex shook his head and continued to drive the jeep forward towards their destination, "You really bought into that crap?"

"Why not?"

"Why not?" Alex explained, "Because it's just a way for them to sell those shitty little volcano models you saw back at the gas station. That's it. Pure and simple. They create this legend, you become more interested. That's how tourism works. They sell you a legend, which is easy to create, and then they capitalise on it with junk to sell. Not being funny but I'm pretty sure someone was saying there has never been an eruption on this island. It's still in dispute as to whether the volcano is even active now… And I'm pretty sure they're not still killing people to satisfy any monsters," he laughed.

"Did you not see that donkey back at the gas station?" the girl argued.

"Seriously?"

"Have you seen that?" the man in the back leaned forward and pointed out towards the beach. "I thought there was supposed to be white sand and turquoise waters? That looks like more of the same to me!"

The jeep slowed to a stop.

"Did we really just pay for this jeep, and fill it with gas, to come to a beach identical to the one we left?" Alex muttered half in disbelief and half in annoyance. His friend in the back started to laugh. "I'm not being funny but I can't be bothered to hang about here for this. We can get this back at the hotel but with the added bonus of free drinks." Alex continued, "Any objections if I just turn us right back around again?"

"None from me," the girl in the passenger seat said.

"Or me," the second girl said.

"We could at least explore through there first," the other lad said, pointing towards the trees. None of the rest of the group were bothered. They'd come out to see a nice beach, not get lost in trees or go climbing mountains. "Or not," he finished when he realised no one else shared the same urge to go exploring.

"At least we know why the jeep is so battered," Alex said as he started to turn it back around again.

"Why?" the girl next to him asked.

"Because…" he turned to her and smiled before slamming his foot down on the accelerator, "… when people realise there's nothing to see or do, they take it off-roading before heading home!"

The jeep climbed the small embankment to the side of the road and landed on the dusty surface of the clearing. Alex pulled the handbrake up and yanked the steering wheel to the left as the two female passengers screamed and his friend cheered him on. The jeep slid to the side before Alex released the handbrake and stamped on the accelerator once more, speeding them towards the trees.

"Slow down!" the girl in the front screamed.

The jeep bounced across the loose surface as the old suspension creaked and groaned with the sudden rough treatment.

"You wanted to see the trees, right?" Alex asked the guy in the back via the rear-view mirror.

"Don't be a prick!" his female passenger screamed.

Alex yanked on the steering wheel again as he pulled the handbrake up once more, causing the vehicle to power slide towards the greenery. It slid to a halt. Alex released the handbrake, revved the engine, and dumped the clutch. The engine roared as the back wheels spun in the earth, kicking up a cloud of dust and stones. Soon they were speeding along the tree-line, the two girls still screaming and the two lads still cheering.

"Look out!" the female in the front screamed as a young woman jumped through the bushes and into the road. Alex slammed on the brakes but all too late and the jeep struck the woman hard before dragging her underneath. The passengers felt the bump bump as both sets of wheels went over the body before the jeep finally slid to a standstill.

No one moved.

No one said anything.

They didn't dare.

Alex looked in the rear-view mirror. His friends, in the back, looked just as shaken as he felt but beyond them - out the back window - he could see the body of a girl. He hesitated a moment, unsure as to whether he should just drive off. Drive off and pretend it had never happened. He wondered whether he'd get away with it. He wondered whether his friends would say anything to anyone if he opted to run. He shook the idea from his head. He couldn't. That's someone's daughter lying back there. Someone's child. He couldn't just leave her there. He opened the door.

"What are you doing?" the girl asked.

"I have to see," he said, shaking.

"Just go," she argued, clearly having had the same thought as him.

Alex ignored her and climbed from the vehicle. The guy in the back also climbed out. As they both nervously approached the girl. Not just any girl but Holly. They could see she was alive. She shouldn't have been. Her limbs were twisted in the wrong direction. A bone sticking out here and a bone sticking out there. Blood leaking from both nostrils and her eyes just as bloodshot. She was trying to say something but words weren't coming out. Just a strange clicking and clacking noise of the tongue, along with the odd pop and bubble of claret red blood. She suddenly breathed in and then slowly exhaled as the soul left her broken body. A low rumble of thunder echoed from the sky as Alex threw up on the ground.

"It's not your fault, mate, it's not your fault!" Alex's friend tried to reassure him. "She just came out of nowhere. She must have known we were there. She must have been able to hear us... It was just an accident..."

"I killed someone…"

"By accident! It was just an accident!"

"What the fuck was she running from to make her leap out like that?" Alex asked as his shock turned to anger. He looked back to where she'd first jumped from the bushes in time to see the tip of the arrow. It sliced through his eye and tore through to his brain. His mouth dropped open and a gargled noise escaped his mouth before he fell forward onto the floor, driving the arrow right through his skull.

His friend turned to see what had happened. There, in the bushes, he saw two natives. One with a painted face and the other with a bow raised, frantically loading a second arrow.

Alex's friend screamed as a low rumble of thunder shook the late afternoon sky.

THE   END

Manufactured by Amazon.ca
Bolton, ON

13843674R00057